TONYA KAPPES

Get Witch
Or
Die Try[

Spies and Spells Myst   series
Book Three

Acknowledgements

This book is dedicated to all my readers who have fallen in love with Mick Jasper and Maggie Park as much as I have!

I want to thank Cyndy Ranzau for the amazing editing. I also want to give a huge shout out to Jessica Fischer for the amazing cover design and bringing the story to life in a photo.

A special thank you to the Kappes Krew, the reviewers, and the bloggers who have helped spread the word about my novels. Without you, there would be no me! You make my dream a reality and I love every minute of it. I hope I do not disappoint you!

And last but not least, I want to thank my very own real life partner, Eddy! He allows me the time I need by keeping up with our boys, fur babies, house work, suppers, and everyday life while I write.

Chapter One

I knew it wasn't going to be a good thing.

As soon as Riule, my mom's cat who also just so happened to be her familiar, jumped up on top of me to get me out of bed this morning, a deep-rooted feeling told me today was not going to go well. I didn't need my witchy instincts to tell me that.

"You aren't doing it right," Mrs. Hubbard said in a dull and troubled voice. She hiked King, her Yorkie, up a little further up on her hip.

Her feisty mood was back, but this time it was on our turf—The Brew's kitchen, our family's retro diner in downtown Louisville, Kentucky—and not out on the green where our house sat across from Mrs. Hubbard's, our very nosy neighbor.

The Brew only served breakfast and lunch, so I was praying the time would go by fast. Real fast.

"I am doing it right," Auntie Meme's voice grated harshly.

She stood over the stove actually using a whisk to stir the ingredients, which was awfully strange to me since Auntie never used a mortal utensil to cook. That alone told me it told me it wasn't going to go well.

Mrs. Hubbard, along with King, stood over her shoulder, which meant that Auntie Meme couldn't just snap her fingers and make everything good or make Mrs. Hubbard disappear, which I was pretty sure was rolling around in her hot-tempered head.

Auntie Meme turned around and came nose-to-nose with Mrs. Hubbard. King's lip quivered as a low growl crept past his gnashed teeth. Auntie's bright red hair stuck up on her head like a dog that was about to pounce on its prey—a stark contrast to Mrs. Hubbard's neatly styled grey chin-length hair and pearls studs in her ears. They eyed each other. Auntie drummed her fingers together. It was only going to take one quick flick and both Mrs. Hubbard and King would go poof. Auntie turned back to the boiling pots on the stove.

I let out a little sigh, thankful that Auntie Meme had backed down. Something that was extremely rare.

Auntie Meme and Mrs. Hubbard have always had the neighbor feud thing going on. Our family diner, The Brew, had always been a safe haven away from our nosy neighbors—at least until I opened my big mouth.

A month or so ago when I was snooping around for Auntie Meme after she'd accused Mrs. Hubbard of stealing a package left by the mailman on our front porch, Mrs. Hubbard had invited me in for a cup of tea and her homemade carrot cake. I was enjoying her cake so much that I'd almost forgotten to look for the package.

This was where my big mouth got us in trouble. I had told my auntie and my mom that I didn't see the package in Mrs. Hubbard's house, but that she'd made the most spectacular little cakes that were so moist. In fact, I raved so much that I'd convinced Auntie Meme that she needed to feature the mini-carrot cakes in the diner for the fall and winter seasons. Mom thought it was a fantastic idea since she needed to keep the prying eyes of Mrs. Hubbard away while she decorated for the Belgravia Court Historic Homes Christmas Tour, which might be sped along by a little magic that might be unexplainable to the mortal eyes.

That brings us to today. Mrs. Hubbard was beyond thrilled to come to the diner and make her cakes with Auntie's help. Plus, Mrs. Hubbard said that her house was falling down around her and she couldn't afford the repairs. She was hoping the money she was going to make from the cake sales at the diner could help her pay for some of the repairs.

Belgravia Court was where we lived in Old Louisville, Kentucky. It's its own quaint little pocket just far enough away from the city to feel like a village with old historic charm. Which was why Mom and Auntie moved our family here. Gosh, Auntie Meme was pushing two-hundred years old and who knew how old Mom was, so the old was just comfortable to them. Which brings me back to the 1890's Victorian homes on Belgravia Court.

Belgravia Court ran for three blocks, with all of the Victorian houses facing each other with a green courtyard running through the middle. The backside of our houses led to an alley on each side where we had our own detached garages. It was truly a magnificent place to live with the charming, gaslight-lantern-lined pathway along the green. It was magical and we didn't have to put a spell on it to make it that way.

Mrs. Hubbard lived across the green with King. Both very nosy and very loud. When Mom talked Auntie into letting Mrs. Hubbard come to The Brew to make her cakes, it was due to the fact that Mom needed a good day's work to prepare the house for the upcoming Belgravia Court Historic Homes Christmas Tour that ran every weekend from the end of November to January. We were only a couple of weeks away and Mom had already been working on this for a month.

Only a few houses were chosen to be included in the exclusive tour and with a little wave of the hand, Mom made sure our house was picked. Mom was competitive and was pulling out all the magic she could muster up to make our house stand out above anyone else's on the tour, which was very strange to me since we spent so much time trying to stay out of sight and blend in with the mortals.

One little problem, Mom didn't have a Christmas decorating bone in her body. She was really good at the other holidays, but for some reason she just couldn't pick one theme or even one century. She had what I called the Christmas flu and our house looked like she'd just vomited decorations everywhere. Yeah, it looks as lovely as it sounds.

Which brings me back to today. Here in the kitchen at The Brew where Auntie Meme was unable to use her magic to whip up her usual daily specials to keep Mrs. Hubbard off of Belgravia Court so Mom could use whatever means necessary to fix the decorated house.

"You need a little more flour, Meme." Mrs. Hubbard was a ticking time bomb as she flinched behind Auntie Meme. King yipped alongside of Mrs. Hubbard.

"Gladys, you need to shut up. You and your ankle bitter are making me nervous." Auntie threw her hands in the air and swiveled around. Her rosy red cheeks were redder than normal; her red hair that normally stuck straight up in the air was flattened with a layer of flour. I could see the spell that was on the tip of her eyelids as her black eyes assessed the situation.

Slowly I shook my head at her. She sucked in a deep breath and rolled her shoulders back.

"I'm sorry, Gladys." It took a lot for Auntie Meme to swallow her witchy pride and not throw a spell on poor old Mrs. Hubbard like she'd done so many times before.

Harmless spells, but spells nonetheless.

"I sure could use some help filling up the salt shakers, Mrs. Hubbard." I knew that if I got Mrs. Hubbard out of the kitchen for even a minute, all would be well and Auntie Meme could do her thing to the carrot cakes.

"Oh that's a great idea." Auntie planted a grip on each side of Mrs. Hubbard's shoulders a little too close to where King was being held. He tried to nip at Auntie's fingers, but quickly stopped after Auntie lifted a finger and sent a little shock to his system. "That way we can hurry up and open so the customers can get in here and taste these delicious treats."

All three of us looked at the cakes just taken out of the oven. They were sunken in the middle. Definitely not fit to feed to a hog, much less a human, mortal or witch.

"I guess we could use a little break," Mrs. Hubbard agreed.

She put King on the floor next to her and scuttled across the floor. She ripped the hairnet off of her grey head of hair. She'd insisted on wearing the hairnet since it was code for the health department, little did she know that the health department had never shown up here thanks to Auntie's flip of the wrist.

She stopped shy of the door between the diner and kitchen. Her eyes darted between Auntie Meme and me as she fiddled with the string of pearls around her neck. She wore her usual uniform of black pants and cardigan. Today's color choice was key-lime green. She tucked a strand of her chin-length hair behind her ear and disappeared into the diner.

I gave Auntie the bright-eyed, hurry-the-heck-up look before I followed Mrs. Hubbard into the dining area.

"Here you go," I said to Mrs. Hubbard.

I reached under the counter and retrieved a refill caddy with all the condiments needed to refill the items on the table.

"Just fill up what you see needs to be done. I'll start over in that corner." I pointed to the window up front. "And work my way around until all the tables are ready to go."

Both of us went in opposite directions.

"I'm glad you are featuring your cakes here. I can't wait to have one." I set the caddy on the retro dining table.

Auntie Meme had fond memories of that time in her life, so when she opened The Brew, she wanted a diner with a black and white tile floor, sparkly vinyl covered metal chairs, and the retro tables to go with it. There was no way I was going to wear the retro outfits she'd originally wanted, so we opted for aprons instead.

"It's a trial run." Mrs. Hubbard's brows rose. "And by the taste of things and look of things, it's only going to be today since she can't seem to get it right." She *tsked*, "How on Earth does she bake and cook all day long and not be able to get a simple cake right?"

"I think she's just trying too hard to perfect your recipe," I replied.

"Well, I was banking on that money to help fix up a few things in my house." There was a worry in her tone that I hadn't heard before.

I kept my head down so she couldn't even try to read the look on my face because I was afraid she was right. If Auntie didn't like how things went today, she wouldn't let Mrs. Hubbard come back. I put a napkin, fork, spoon, knife, and frosted plastic cup in front of each chair at each table. My head jerked up when I noticed a shadow of a person cast into the diner from the outside morning sun just starting to peek over the buildings in downtown where the diner was located.

The person wore a black round-brim hat that covered the eyes. It must've been a customer looking to see if we were open because they took off when I looked up. I shrugged it off and went about my chores of filling up the items on the table, but when Vinnie whizzed by, I paused, rubbing my hand over my red dangling crystal necklace.

Vinnie is my 1964 AC Cobra and also my familiar. I know he's not the regular familiar that mortals have gotten used to seeing in the movies and books, but that's how little mortals really knew about the real witchy world.

Vinnie had a mind of his own and kept me safe. When he sped off from where he'd parked this morning it made my stomach curl. My necklace didn't warm (the usual sign of danger) nor did I get any witchy sense that something was wrong.

The rattle of pans and a loud crash, sort of sounding like a mini-explosion, was followed up by a puff of flour bursting through the window between the kitchen and diner, leaving me with little time to think about Vinnie.

"Oh, lordy." Mrs. Hubbard shook her head, her tongue heavy with sarcasm.

"Auntie Meme?" I called out. "Are you okay?"

The cloud of flour settled and she popped her head through the window. Her hair no longer had even a speck of white flour in it as it had when Mrs. Hubbard and I were in the kitchen with her, nor did she look ruffled.

"I'm happier than a puppy with two tails." The smile on her face told me that she'd done a little magic while I'd occupied Mrs. Hubbard. Her hands lifted up a tray of the most beautiful little carrot cakes that looked exactly like Mrs. Hubbard's.

"Knock me down and steal muh teeth!" Mrs. Hubbard's eyes popped open at the sight of the cakes on the tray. "How on Earth did you get those baked so quickly?" Mrs. Hubbard giddy-upped on over to the window and peered at the cakes that were as pretty as a picture. "And you frosted them exactly how I do it," she said.

Her tone set off alarm bells ringing in my head. Auntie Meme had to be really careful. Mrs. Hubbard was one smart old bird.

I walked over and took the plate of small cakes from Auntie and put them underneath the glass dome on the counter to display.

"Well? How did you do it so fast?" Mrs. Hubbard wasn't going to be satisfied with the silence Auntie Meme had given her.

"You made me nervous looking over my shoulder." Auntie Meme clicked the heels of her black boots and twirled around on the balls of her feet. Her shoes clicked against the black and white tile of the kitchen floor. "And that's why I actually own and cook at my own diner," Auntie Meme was both excited and aggravated.

"She is good." I tucked a piece of my long black hair behind my ear as I tried to avoid Mrs. Hubbard's eyes and smooth the less than believable explanation Auntie Meme had given her.

"Good?" Mrs. Hubbard questioned. "Something ain't right. It takes at least a good hour to cool one of them small cakes and ice it. That doesn't even include the baking time. There's no way we've been out here for more than five minutes, much less an hour." Mrs. Hubbard glanced back at the kitchen window before her eyes shifted back to me. She shook her finger at me. "I know something fishy is going on because I know your car wasn't parked there when we walked out here."

My eyes followed her finger. Vinnie's alarm was going off.

"Auntie!" I screamed across the diner's dining room.

"What?" Her head popped out of the kitchen window.

"I. . ." I pointed over my shoulder. Her eyes flew open. "Go!" She gestured.

The red gem warmed against my skin. My gut dropped.

Chapter Two

"Maggie, I think you might be in danger," Vinnie's voice was bold and to the point.

"That's a fine way to greet me." I looked at the diner where Mrs. Hubbard was staring at me. "Plus you put on a *real* good show for Mrs. Hubbard."

"I'm sorry, Maggie." He put his gear shift in drive and peeled out of the space. "I am here to keep you safe from harm and when that person with the mysterious hat was looking through The Brew's window, my circuits went off. I followed them down the street only they ducked down the alleyway. By the time I made it around the building, they were gone."

"I saw them looking through the window, but I figured they were looking at what time we opened." I put my hands on his wheel to appear as if I was driving in case someone looked over.

"I didn't like what I felt, Maggie. I think it's best you go home and help your mother out with the Christmas decorations." He tried to make a left to go toward home, but I flipped on his manual switch. "Maggie, what are you doing?"

"I understand that you want me to be safe and home is probably the best place. But, there's no way in broomsticks that I'm going to help Mom decorate for Christmas when she completely skipped decorating for Halloween and Thanksgiving since she entered our house into the Christmas tour. Besides," I braced myself because I knew he was going to blow a gasket when he heard what I was going to say next, "I need to go to SKUL and get my paycheck."

Immediately, Vinnie slowed down to a snail's crawl.

"Seriously?" I pushed the gas pedal a little more, which didn't do much for me. Even in manual mode, there were limits. I did have full control of the steering wheel. "If it takes me all day to get there, I'm still going."

"Maggie, Mick Jasper has not contacted you for a couple of months. You will get your check another day. I think it's in your best interest to go home. I think your mother would agree." Vinnie wasn't happy with my Life's Journey, but it wasn't for him to approve.

"If your hunch is right about that person, the only way to find out if something is going on is to make an appearance at SKUL," I said knowing that SKUL and my Life's Journey were tied together.

Every witch had what was called a Life's Journey, what their purpose on this earth was. It wasn't until the last six months that I'd found out my Life's Journey was to be an undercover civilian agent for SKUL, Secret Keepers of Universal Law. As a part of Interpol it was a big spy division to keep the United States a safe place.

And I'd worked a couple of cases with them as a civilian who they claimed blended into society. They had no clue that I was a witch and I would blend in just about anywhere with a snap of my fingers. Regardless, I still had a paycheck coming to me and it was a great way to see if there was really something going on or if Vinnie and I were just a little too on edge.

"You wait right here until I get back," I warned Vinnie even though he had a mind of his own and did what he thought was in my best interest. I grabbed my SKUL badge and put it in my pocket.

When I got out of the car, I looked back at him with a scowl to let him know to play the normal, everyday car part. Like a good familiar, he beeped as though he had locked his doors, when in reality he didn't need to lock a door because if anyone tried to mess with him, they'd get the surprise of their life.

"Good morn—" Patsy looked up from the receptionist desk. SKUL headquarters was disguised as a dental office. It even came with the smell of cement and fluoride. "Oh, it's you." Her lips pursed.

"Good morning, Patsy." I smiled and showed her my badge.

"Wait right there." She stood up and stopped me from going around her to the hallway that led to the secret door to an elevator. "Does Mick know you are coming because he didn't say anything to me."

Mick Jasper. I sighed.

There were many reasons Vinnie didn't like my Life's Journey, one reason in particular. Mick Jasper.

She grabbed the receiver of her phone and started to punch numbers.

"I'm not here to see Mick. I'm here to see Burt." I pushed my way around her desk but not without giving her a bout of upset stomach with the wiggle of my nose.

A loud gurgle came from her belly. She blinked. One hand held the receiver while the other one clutched her stomach. She gulped a couple of times and rolled her lips together.

"You stay." She stuck her hand in front of her and scurried past me, putting her hand over her mouth.

"If only you'd learn and let me back without an issue," I whispered and helped myself down the hall.

I opened the door that hid the elevator and got in once its doors slid open. I pushed the button to the bottom floor where the guts and inner workings of SKUL was located. The sound of people typing, talking, and the shuffling of papers filled the room around the cubicles. All different SKUL agents working on different things.

I nodded to a few people who had recognized me and I recognized from the few times I'd been there. I walked down the hall to Burt's office. Burt Devlin was the head of SKUL and the one who saw my potential value add to the team. Albeit, I'd yet to have the formal training he said I'd get, but so far my only duties were to blend in and see what I could overhear or uncover while feeding all the information to Mick Jasper.

Mick Jasper. My heart did a little flutter when I saw him sitting in the chair in Burt's office through the glass wall of windows. I'm a sucker for tall, dark and muscular, but it's his blue eyes that are killer and jabbed me right in the heart and weakened my knees.

I opened the door and realized clearly I was interrupting something. Something I'd describe as evil.

"I'm sorry," I apologized and took a step back out the door while holding on to the door knob. "I'll just wait outside," I said to all six eyes that seemed surprised to see me.

Burt leaned up against his desk with his arms crossed. Mick sat in the chair in front of him and Sherry, another SKUL agent who usually worked with Mick, was sitting down on the couch in the back of the room.

"No, no." Burt waved me in. "Come on in. Funny you are here. I was actually going to call you today."

"To give me my check?" I asked.

"That too, but we were just discussing the deaths of two local women," he said.

"You mean those girls on the news?" I asked before I stepped back into the room and shut the door behind me.

Suddenly I'd taken an interest, not that I was going to have any answers. I'd seen a little snip of it on the news but didn't pay much attention to it. There were shootings all over the city. It was on the news nightly and had become one of those things you expected to hear, like the weather forecast.

"They have one thing in common." Burt stood up and walked around the desk.

"And what might that be?" I asked, being nosy.

"Me." Mick stood up and rolled down the sleeves of his blue button down. His brows rose. "Let's say I dated them at one time or another."

"Unfortunately, there is no other tie between the women and the police are looking into Mick." Burt pushed the file on his desk toward the edge.

"May I?" I asked to see what was inside.

"Sir." Sherry stepped forward. "No offense, but Maggie doesn't have clearance and she certainly isn't going to be on the case."

"No offense taken." I put my hands up and totally wished I could give her a zit the size of a quarter on her chin or make her have an onset of grey hair that no amount of dye could cover for a few months.

"I think that Maggie has fresh eyes and I like using her as a consultant." Burt pushed it further toward me.

"You're the boss." Sherry took the file and handed it to me. "The only thing in there are photos of the women and their information. One was a nurse's aide and the other was a paralegal. Both from opposite sides of the tracks." Sherry glanced over at Mick.

"What?" He rolled his eyes. "I don't discriminate on the women I've dated."

"I bet you don't." Sherry shook her head with a chuckle. "The only thing Mick does have going for him is that he has alibis for both murders."

"That's why we think someone is trying to frame Mick," Burt said.

"But why me?" Mick walked over to the window and looked out. "Ummm, Maggie. Your car is rolling."

I let out an audible groan.

"Sir, let me look at the file and I'll get back to you tomorrow." I grabbed the file and ran out the door.

I don't know why I did it and I knew better but I continued to tap the up button on the elevator as if that was going to hurry it up. I glanced around and no one seemed to be looking. I dragged my finger under my nose and instantly appeared in the corner of the lobby.

"Where did you come from?" Patsy's head turned side-to-side. Her mouth dropped.

"I slipped by you." I headed to the door.

"Here is your check." She waved an envelope in the air.

I snatched it on my way past her.

"Thanks. I hope you feel better," I said and darted out the door.

Vinnie was exactly where I'd left him.

"What on Earth did you do that for?" I asked in a snippy voice after I got in and he slammed the door behind me.

"Maggie, you said that you were only going to be a few minutes and it was much longer than that. I was beginning to worry." He started his engine. I flipped on his automatic switch. "When I saw Agent Jasper looking out the window, I knew if I moved he'd make some sort of comment about your old car, which by the way I do not like being referred to as old. My pistons and gears are lubed better than his insides."

"You have to be careful. You can't let anyone know that you are not a normal car." I opened the file and took a long look at the woman staring back at me from the first photo.

She was probably younger than me by a few years, which didn't surprise me. I could see Mick dating younger women. Which seemed to be true by looking at the women.

Both of them had very pretty smiles that showed off brilliant white teeth, yet the way they dressed said a lot about their personalities. One was in a pant suit while the other was in jeans, tee, and Chucks.

"Maggie, Agent Jasper believes I'm an old car and that strange things go on with me." Vinnie drove much faster home than he did going to SKUL, which didn't surprise me. "Besides, Agent Jasper is none of my concern. You are."

"SKUL is my Life's Journey, which means that Mick Jasper is part of it too." I dragged my finger down the paper to check out the occupations of the women.

One of them was a legal secretary and the other was a nurse's aide in a nursing home. Their birthdays were different, not even the same birth months. Their cars were completely different. The secretary drove a four-door Toyota, the nurse's aide drove a motorcycle. They even lived on opposite sides of town. They had nothing in common, well. . .nothing except Mick Jasper.

"Maggie?" Vinnie asked. "I've been parked in the garage for a few minutes now and you haven't even noticed we made it home."

I glanced up.

"Not that Burt has asked me to be on the case, but he did ask me to look at the file to see if there was anything that stood out." I looked up and over the wheel. "You know, Vinnie, there is nothing that stands out to me."

"That makes me want to protect you more from Agent Jasper. Because of him you've been at gun point twice in the last six months." Vinnie reminded me of worse times.

"It doesn't hurt to look into some things." I shut the folder and ran a finger over my necklace.

"What is it Maggie?" Vinnie asked.

"I don't know, Vinnie. Something is off about this. I know Mick Jasper is not a killer, but someone is trying to make it look like he did kill them." I bit my lip and let out a sigh.

The twinkling Christmas lights from the kitchen window caught my attention.

"How do you know that Agent Jasper didn't do it?" Red dots waved across Vinnie's circuit board screen.

"The police have established an alibi for Mick." Mentally I prepared myself for the winter wonderland I was about to walk into.

"He is a SKUL agent. He has a lot of contacts and he knows a lot of people." Vinnie always looked at things from all angles, only when it came to Mick, the angle was always negative.

"You think he actually had these women knocked off?" A chuckle escaped me. "Why would he do that?"

"They know something about him." Vinnie wasted no time in responding. "He had dated them. They knew him in a more intimate situation and he might've told them something that was classified.

"He found out and realized what he'd told them and for the information not to come out, he killed them." Vinnie's words drifted off and I jumped when a pumpkin flew out the back door of my house before the door slammed shut. "I've got to go."

"Anything is possible, Maggie," Vinnie said before I got out of the car. "You remember that now that you are part of the mortal world."

Chapter Three

"Mortal world," I murmured under my breath and looked at the smashed pumpkin lying on the concrete patio next to the pool.

Riule crawled out from underneath Mom's herb garden.

Mom was in a mood and it was much easier to prepare for it before I walked in.

"What's going on?" I asked Riule, my mom's black cat and familiar. I bent down and rubbed my hand down his back.

"She's had a rough day getting into the Christmas spirit," Riule meowed back in words to my ears but to the mortal ears, he was simply acting like a cat.

"We are witches." I couldn't help but grin before feeling sorry for him. "You've had to listen to her all day?"

"All day. She's yelling Riule this, Riule that." He rolled his little green eyes. "When she asks for my opinion, I can't help but throw in something that is black in color and she flies off, literally." I knew he what he meant.

Mom was good at jumping on her broom when the going got tough. Sometimes she'd disappear for days. It might sound a bit harsh for a mom to take off, but in our case it was good because it was time for her to cool down and not just up and move all of us like she'd done when me and Lilith were kids.

"She screams that Christmas is green and red, not black." He shook his head.

A crash came from the house. In a flash, Riule had run back under the bushes.

"Mom! We are witches not elves!" Lilith's voice exploded out of the open kitchen window.

"Not an elf!" Gilbert, Lilith's rare purple macaw familiar, echoed Lilith's displeasure.

It was time to face the music. I couldn't stay outside forever. I tucked the file under my arm and walked in through the back door, which led straight into the kitchen where Mom, Auntie Meme and Lilith were having a standoff.

"Finally," Mom threw her arms in the air. "A voice of reason." She pointed to me. I turned to look behind me and, seeing no one, pointed to myself.

"Me?" I looked between the three of them. "What do you have on?" I asked Mom after my eyes settled on her green shoes that were curled up on the toe with a bell on it.

There was a tinsel hat on top of Lilith's head. Her bangs flattened on her forehead.

"I'm dressed as an elf to help work on the creative vision." As Mom rotated her wrist in a circle, little sparks flew out.

"You can't just 'poof' and 'piff'?" Auntie Meme asked with Miss Kitty, her owl familiar, perched on her shoulder. "Like this. Poof." She lifted her right hand and then her left. A tiny lit and decorated Christmas tree appeared in her right hand. "Piff," she said and a small laughing Santa appeared in her left hand.

"No," Mom gasped and pointed a finger at Auntie Meme, zapping the Santa and disintegrating him into a pile of ashes. "I want to do this the mortal way."

Miss Kitty spread her wings and lifted into the air, hovering over Mom like she did when Auntie Meme used her to cast a spell.

"This is ridiculous." I stood between them. I curled my nose at Miss Kitty and didn't stop until she floated back down to land on Auntie's shoulder. "Mom, you are the one who signed up for this Christmas tour." I turned to Lilith. "Lilith is right. We are witches. We love Christmas and all that goes with it, but it doesn't come as natural as carving a pumpkin or flying." I pointed to her broom that was propped up against the table. "We need to just regroup, have some spiced brew and get a plan." I nodded toward everyone.

"If you think I'm dressing up like an elf to help your mom's creative flow, then you have another thing coming," Auntie Meme warned. "Besides, what have you been doing all day while I entertained Gladys?"

Mom's body shifted to the left and she stuck her fists on her hips.

"I had to put up with her annoying laugh, yappy dog, and if I had to hear her tell one more customer how she created the cakes and brag on and on about her nephew, I was going to turn her into a toad." Auntie Meme took a step toward Mom. "Now tell me, while I kept her prying eyes out of view of the house, what did you do all day?"

Auntie Meme was on edge. It was a tall order for Mom to ask her to keep Mrs. Hubbard busy so she could decorate without Mrs. Hubbard's nosy spying. I'd seen it with my own eyes. Mrs. Hubbard's family room had a perfect view of our house and into our house. She even had a pair of binoculars sitting on the floor next to her chair.

I spoke up, "I'm just saying that maybe each of us can help Mom out somehow. She's always been there for us." I tried so hard to be the voice of reason.

There was a lot of nods, *um huhs*, and *yeps* coming from Mom's lips.

"Have you forgotten that just a few months ago she wanted you to marry a mortal because she never thought you'd find your Life's Journey and tried to set you up with

Abram Callahan?" Just the sound of Abram's name made my stomach hurt.

Abram was, well had been, a longtime family friend who grew up with me on Belgravia Court. We were best friends up until recently and he'd wanted to take it to a much deeper level. Abram knew there was something special about our family after I'd brought back Boomer, his cat, to life a few times over the course of our childhood and into adulthood. Abram was a local mechanic we used to work on Vinnie. He was good at keeping his mouth shut. Unfortunately, a few months ago we had to do a memory erasing spell on him because he was getting a little too comfortable knowing our family secret and we just couldn't trust he'd keep our secret for life.

We worked very hard at keeping our real life on the down low and I wasn't about to let one guy ruin it for us. Auntie Meme had been the target of many witch hunts in her life and she said she was too old to go through another one.

"Okay, I'll give you Abram." The memory was still too fresh in my mind. "But we must move on. The season has changed, the old have died, and it's our time of the year for renewal." I recited the words of a seasonal spell. "So we are all we have and we need to help each other out."

"When did you get all high and witchy?" Lilith glared at me and ripped the hat off of her head.

"Really?" I tilted my head to the side. "I'm trying to keep the peace and keep our family secret safe."

Mom lifted her chin and took a couple of deep breaths as if she were trying to keep from crying.

"Fine." Lilith's words stuck like a sword. "I'll help but I won't dress up."

"Yes you will." Auntie dragged her hand down her body. "But I'm going to be the big guy."

I tried not to laugh when a Santa outfit appeared on her body. Her natural rosy cheeks and short red hair reminded me of the children's Christmas cartoon *Santa Claus Is Coming To Town*. She looked like the young Kris Kringle.

"What?" She cocked a brow.

"Okay, Mom." Lilith had completely decided to be a sexy elf, giving me sister envy. "What can we do?"

"I really want to try to put up a Christmas tree in all of the rooms, but by hand, and I don't mean wave of the hand." At least Mom continued to stay true to her word.

It would be so much easier to wave a hand, snap a finger, wrinkle a nose to do dishes, make a bed, sweep the floor, but Mom has always insisted we did the mortal thing. She took pride in fitting and blending in. Me. . .not so much. What was the point of having these great talents and not using them?

I did use them at SKUL when I could. Unfortunately, unlike what mortals thought, we couldn't just get ourselves out of any situation with a wink of an eye. That's the downside. It depended on the situation and that was why we had familiars, to help us out in tight situations.

"All the trees are in boxes in the family room," Mom called over her shoulder and we followed her down the hall. "I have each box labeled for each room."

The boxes were stacked high to the ceiling.

"Where did you get all of these trees?" I asked.

"Maybe I did a teeny-tiny bit of magic." Her fingers mocked the teeny-tiny she was talking about. "I'm the mom. You can't use magic. Only use creativity the mortal way."

Lilith and I rolled our eyes before we each took a box. Instead of dragging a box upstairs, since Mom wouldn't let me snap it up to my room, I decided to do the tree in the family room.

"How did the diner go today?" I asked Auntie as she dragged her finger down the boxes.

"Pleased to say that Gladys's carrot cakes sold out." She glanced over her shoulder, and then tapped the box, letting it float out of the pile and into the entryway.

"You are brave." I smiled. "Not only decorating the tree the tourists are going to see first, but using a little magic." I winked.

"Shhh." She returned the grin.

Auntie Meme and I had a special bond. She was my guardian for my Life's Journey, which wasn't a surprise to me since we'd been close all of my life. Even as a child when Mom forbid her to help me with any chores. Where Mom made me do them as a mortal, Auntie Meme would appear and wiggle her nose or give a special wink to help me out. She was a lot of fun.

"I'm not going to try to sugar coat it, her cakes were a big hit," Auntie said.

"You put the spell on them." I recalled the little stunt she pulled when Mrs. Hubbard and I had gone to refill the condiments on the tables.

"I didn't put a spell on them, I made them using my own cooking techniques." She waved her hand at the box and toward the entryway, allowing it to float the path, of which I was in the way. When the box passed me, an elf hat appeared on my head. Auntie Meme giggled.

"You and I both know what that means." I opened the box and was happy to see Mom had picked a snowman theme for the family room. I loved a good snowman.

There was a knock on the front door. Auntie Meme and I looked at each other. We weren't expecting company. We never expected company. She shrugged, we snapped our fingers and had the rooms completely decorated before she opened the door.

"Mick," Auntie Meme put her hands together in delight. "Come on in."

Mick? My mind reeled as to why he was there.

"Ho, ho, ho." Joy bubbled in Mick's voice. "Merry Christmas, Santa. Am I on the nice list or naughty?"

"We will see about that. Happy Thanksgiving." Auntie Meme pulled the door wide open.

"It's not quite Thanksgiving yet, but by the looks of it, you are just skipping it and going right on into Christmas," he said with amusement and followed up with a sexy, deep laugh.

I walked into the entryway to stop him from coming deeper into the house.

"Mick." I planted a smile on my face, but my insides were dying. He was already immune to any sort of spell because he was part of my Life's Journey.

Actually, a spell I tried on him from me losing a friendly game of Truth or Spell between me and Lilith at The Derby, a neighborhood bar which sounded really good about now, had gone wrong. I was supposed to put a temporary cat spell on Mick when it bounced off of him and hit the wrong fellow. That's when I knew my Life's Journey had to do with Mick Jasper, only I didn't know it was with SKUL until a few days later. Here we were today.

He was very good looking and pretty damn hot, but at a distance. I couldn't put my heritage at risk for a fling with a mortal, not that he thought of me in that way.

"Book club?" He pointed to my head where I'd forgotten about the elf hat.

I dragged it off my head. "No book club tonight. Mom has entered the house into the Belgravia Court Historic Homes Christmas Tour."

Auntie Meme had a group of witch friends called the Spell Circle. They got together and created new spells, or even just did cleansing spells in full witch regalia: pointy toe heeled boots, black dresses, hats and all. Mick always had the perfect timing of showing up when the Spell Circle was meeting and in order to explain their dress code, I lied and said it was her book club and they dressed to align with the book's theme because he didn't need to know who we really were.

"Oh, I thought you might be reading *The Night Before Christmas*." He laughed and rolled back on his heels. "Hey, Maggie, can I talk to you?"

"Sure," I moved past Auntie Meme and her prying smile, grabbing him by the elbow and dragging him out as fast as I could onto the front porch.

The nip in the late afternoon air tickled across my collar bones and I wished I had on a light jacket. October weather in Kentucky was a bit chilly in the mornings and nights but a bit warmer in the afternoon. It was a tad bit early for the breeze to hold a chill, which told me cold weather was coming and coming fast.

An twinge in my soul told me that we were being watched through Mrs. Hubbard's binoculars, so I positioned us behind one of the pillars on our front porch.

"I wanted to make sure you knew that I didn't kill those girls." The corners of Mick's eyes dropped.

"I know you didn't." Well, I didn't know, but I had a hunch. "It really doesn't matter what I think."

"Sure it does." Mick put his warm hand on my arm. He peeled off his black leather coat and wrapped it around my shoulders. "You're cold."

"Thanks." I pulled the edges of the collar closer and kept it fisted. "I'm going to help out if Burt will let me."

"No, I mean, I don't want you," he touched the front of his jacket on my chest, "to think I did this."

My stomach twitched.

"I don't date any and every girl that comes my way." He stepped back and down a step. He cocked his right foot on the top step and leaned his forearm down on his thigh. He had on a pair of khaki pants and a blue-and-white-striped, long-sleeved polo with a pair of Sperry loafers. A typical southern outfit for a Kentucky man on a fall day. "I'm very selective about who knows me and who I date. They didn't even know what I do for a living."

"Okay." Inside I cringed because I couldn't come up with a better word than *okay*.

He straightened up when a group of people walked down the courtyard on Belgravia Court and turned right on St. James Street heading toward Central Park where the annual St. James Art Festival was in full swing.

"They must be going to the festival." I didn't recognize the group, which meant they didn't live on Belgravia Court and were probably just looking around at our beautiful slice of heaven.

"I'm headed that way to see an old high school friend," he said.

Mrs. Hubbard's front door opened and King came charging out of the house yipping and yapping at the tourists walking on the other side of the black wrought iron fence on the side of Mrs. Hubbard's house.

It was an ornamental fence that gave Belgravia Court a border between us and the outside walkway of St. James Street.

"Hi, Maggie," Mrs. Hubbard called. There was a young man standing next to her. "This is my nephew visiting from New York. He's a fancy art dealer."

I squeezed a smile on my face and waved.

"I was telling him about the diner and he's going to meet me there tomorrow for lunch." Pride rolled across her face with each bounce she made on the balls of her feet.

I nodded again with the same stupid grin on my face. Auntie Meme was going to love this.

"Say," Mick rubbed his hands together and turned my attention back to him. "Want to walk down with me?"

"Right now?" I asked.

"Yeah." His blue eyes tugged at my heart.

"So we can discuss the case?" I asked.

"No. Just us going to look at the art," he said. "And to meet up with my friend."

"Sure." My heart raced under his jacket. I took it off my shoulders to keep my trembling hands busy. I had no idea what was going on with me because no man had ever made me feel this way and it was new to me. I handed him his coat. "Let me get my coat."

He stepped up on the step as if he were going to follow me. I opened the door.

"I'll be right back." I turned to him and held up a finger.

I leaned up against the shut door and closed my eyes trying to let the feeling pass.

"Ummhmmmm," Auntie Meme hummed. "Yep. Your Life's Journey is going to get you in trouble in more ways than one."

I opened my eyes and looked at her. I hesitated, torn by conflicting emotions.

Chapter Four

Mick and I followed right behind the crowd on the sidewalk of St. James Street as we made our way down to the festival with the leaves crunching under our feet. The sun was going down and the brisk air nipped at the top of my ankle boots where my skin was exposed from my ankle jeans. I'd put a green waist-length cloak around my shoulders over my black turtleneck, which kept most of the breeze off of me.

The leaves on the hundred-year-old trees were turning into a canopy of yellows, oranges, and light greens. It was truly a beautiful sight and I wasn't just talking about Mick.

"This thing gets bigger every year." Mick cautiously looked around the street and into the park where there were rows and rows of white tents next to each other.

One after the other displaying their fine art to contribute to the festival.

"There does seem to be a lot of people here." I lifted my hand and pressed on the red jewel necklace dangling from my neck that was tucked under my shirt.

The way things were going, I couldn't be too cautious around Mick if someone was trying to set him up or if he really had killed those women.

We moseyed from tent to tent, trying to get a look at what everyone had to sell. Most of the items were crafted in Kentucky. There were many booths with canvas paintings of Churchill Downs, Keeneland, Kentucky basketball, along with handmade jewelry, shirts, and scarves.

I lingered a little too long at the homemade soap tent because when I turned around Mick was nowhere to be found and looking for him in this crowd would be virtually impossible. At least I thought that until my phone's text alert rang from my back pocket. Mick had made his way over to the amphitheater where the headliners for the festival were located.

I took my time getting over there so I wouldn't seem so eager to see him. If he was a killer, he was a mighty fine looking one and I didn't mind the staring eyes of the women as we'd walked by and their stare ended on me.

Unfortunately, when I walked up on the stage of the amphitheater, he was in the arms of another woman. They were embraced in a more than friendly sort of way and I couldn't tell from her long brown ponytail what she looked like because her face was buried against Mick's chest. Chiseled chest. And the only reason I knew that was because I'd been to his apartment before when he'd changed shirts.

She reminded me of a typical artist with a paint brush stuck through the band holding up her ponytail and her bohemian dress that flowed around her. They were locked in their hug in front of the exhibit for the famous painter, Angela Fritz, who was the headliner of the festival. I'd heard at our last Belgravia Court meeting that the St. James Art Festival committee had a hard time getting her to come because her schedule was full. Apparently the old woman had a lot of money because she lived in Paris, as in France not Kentucky, for half of the year. Much of that time was spent as a recluse. She didn't do many interviews and was always able to avoid the paparazzi. In an interview she'd done for the festival, I read that she claimed her art spoke for itself and her image shouldn't reflect that, which was why her contract was written that she was not to be photographed. Which in today's society was probably pretty hard with cell phones and security cameras planted everywhere.

"Maggie," Mick said as he and the amazingly beautiful brown-haired woman parted.

She was intimidatingly gorgeous and she didn't need hair to enhance her features. Her eyes were slightly shaped in cat eyes and lined perfectly. Lilith would've loved to compare notes with this woman since Lilith worked for Mystic Couture, a very famous and popular makeup line.

"Don't tell me." The woman pointed to my face.

Did I know her? She was smiling so big that it was contagious. She snapped, pointed, and snapped again. I couldn't help but be a little envious of the lipstick mark she'd put on Mick.

"Jockey Red. Mystic Couture." She folded her arms proudly across her more than ample breasts, slightly tucking in the wavy dress to show off her petite figure. There was a bit of pride on her face.

"How did you know?" I asked in a little bit of a shock when she named my favorite color of lipstick that I always wore and never strayed from. I should've known someone who seemed as sophisticated as her would know Mystic Couture.

"It's my favorite. But today I'm wearing Pumpkin Ginger from Mystic Couture because they'd left me a package in my suite at the hotel." She untangled her arms and held her thin hand toward me. "I'm Angela Fritz."

Apparently not an old woman. I had to work really hard to not have my mouth gape open.

"Where are my manners?" Mick shook his head like he had to shake off the lipstick marks on his cheeks. "Angela, this is my friend, Maggie." He turned to me and pointed to the infamous Fritz painting called *The Ville*. "That is the painting which made her famous."

"Friend?" Lightly we shook hands while she inspected me. "Why, Mick Jasper, have you been keeping something from little ole me?"

"Never, my love." He wrapped her in his arms, pulling her hand from mine and giving her another big bear hug.

She giggled in delight and I tried not to puke on her right there. I desperately wanted her to look a tad bit ugly or even a little smudge on the toe of her fancy black shoes would've helped. But Angela Fritz was almost as perfect as an eighty degree, no humidity summer day in the bluegrass state.

"We are just friends. In fact, Maggie lives on Belgravia Court." His brows wiggled.

"Oh my gawd!" Her southern drawl dripped off her words. "Remember how we used to say we were going to live there, but we could never afford it."

"I could never afford it and still can't. You on the other hand." Mick sucked in a deep breath. "Damn, it's so good to see you."

"Well, well, well." A shifty male's voice chimed in.

He stood about six-foot-three, his head bald from hair, but not from a complete tattoo that looked like a cowboy hat. Even though it was chilly out, this man didn't seem to mind as his big, huge, muscled arms burst out of the homemade sleeveless white shirt that was so tight, I could make out the outline of his pecs. The tattoo sleeves left not even a speck of skin on his arms bare, instead they were colored up with bucking horses, lassos, cowboy boots and even a big-boobied woman with only a cowboy hat on her long flowing locks. He was stocky and big.

"I knew if I came down here, I'd find you two just like I did back in school. Always hanging out in the amphitheater trying to hide a forty-ouncer." He hooked his thumbs on the belt loops of his skin tight blue jeans and rocked back on the heels of his authentic cowboy boots.

"Big Stevenson." Angela quickly dumped Mick and held her arms out to the man. She put her hand flat on his chest and instead of a kiss on the cheek, she planted a kiss right on Big's lips.

There was a bit of uncomfortable silence between Mick and me as we tried not to look, but it was difficult. There was definitely some chemistry between Big and Angela. Mick shifted uneasily on his feet from side-to-side.

"How are you, my big lug?" She affectionately looked at him with her head tilted far back.

It was Big Stevenson who backed away from her first. She had a little disappointed look on her face and when she saw that I was looking at her, she grinned and went back to the bubbly and gorgeous artist on display for everyone to gawk at.

"I've been busier than a one-legged man in a butt-kickin' contest." His eyes narrowed and as a genuine grin crossed his lips, he winked. "How 'bout you, darlin'?"

"Don't you darlin' me." She tapped her fingernail on his chest. "I spent many years trying to get in touch with you, but you were all over this country riding bulls."

"Stevenson," I said and nodded, vaguely remembering a famous rodeo cowboy from this area. "You're the rodeo guy."

"That would be my good friend." Mick stepped up as if he'd gotten lost and had just caught up in the conversation. "Big and Angela were an item back in the day. He kept a pretty tight leash on her."

"Hell," Big bent over to my height, "if I didn't, you were going to try to wrangle my little woman."

"Well, I'm not your woman now." She flirted between the two men.

"You are a famous art-teest." Big teased before he smacked her right on the derriere and she jumped.

She held up a finger when a woman walked over to her and whispered in her ear. When they pulled away, she looked over his shoulder. There was a long line at her table of people waiting to get her autograph on one of the very expensive paintings she had for sale.

"Say, fellas." She turned back around. "Why don't we meet for a drink tomorrow night at my hotel with a little dinner in my room to reminisce about old times while I'm in town? I've got some people I need to see tonight, but tomorrow would be great because I have to skedaddle the next day."

Both Mick and Big looked about half stupid with their tongues practically wagging out of their mouths as they nodded.

"I don't have much to do. I came here to see you." Big was much larger than Mick when they stood side-by-side. He was definitely thicker in the shoulders and arms. He had real pretty blue eyes.

Mick looked at me.

"Oh, you can come too, Maggie," Angela spoke up. "The more the merrier."

The young brunette lightly touched Angela's elbow to get her to hurry.

"Listen," she pouted and turned to the waiting fans, "I've got to get going. I'm in the penthouse of the Galt House. Come by around seven pm tomorrow night so we can catch up."

She didn't wait for an answer. She simply assumed they'd, we'd, be there and blew kisses at each of them before she greeted her awaiting public.

"She looks good, doesn't she?" Big smiled as if he'd still had the prize after all of these years.

"Yep. You should've held on to that one." Mick smacked Big on the back.

"So what are you doing nowadays?" he asked Mick. "I see who you're doing it with." He winked at me.

"I do a little bit here and there for Dad." Mick lied. He started to explain what a little bit of what this and that was but I lost his voice when my necklace warmed against my chest.

I glanced around and out of the corner of my eye, I saw someone in a black round-brim hat pulled down, covering their eyes facing me from the corner of the stage before they quickly turned the corner and disappeared.

"Excuse me." I didn't wait for Big or Mick to answer since they seemed to be in some sort of contest one-upping each other. Though I could feel Mick's stare.

It seemed that he knew me a little better each time we worked together, so he knew when I was onto something. This man might not have had anything to do with what was going on with Mick, but it was the second time I'd seen him today and that was not coincidental. Especially when my necklace warmed. It was Vinnie's way of telling me that danger was lurking.

I rounded the corner of the amphitheater, which faced Fourth Street in time to catch the person disappearing into a waiting cab. I put my hands on my hips and faced the back of the cab as it zoomed down Fourth and headed toward Magnolia when a toot of a very familiar horn sounded behind me.

I let out a sigh of relief when I saw it was Vinnie pulling up to the curb. I scurried around his hood as he opened his door, but not without hearing Mick calling my name.

"What are you doing? Where did your car come from?" Mick questioned.

"Get in!" I jumped in the front seat and fastened my seatbelt.

Vinnie took off with one of Mick's feet still hanging out of the passenger side door.

"Slow down." Mitch held on for dear life. "What is going on?"

"I don't know." I kept my hands on Vinnie's wheel like I was doing all the driving when in reality I was only letting Vinnie follow the cab. "All I know is that I have seen the same person twice in one day looking at me. Once at The Brew and once just now."

"So you are chasing them?" Mick made it sound like I had lost my mind.

"Think about it, Mick." I gripped the wheel as Vinnie crossed Hill Street. "This person could be the killer and after me since you and I have spent some time together. I might be next on the list. They might think we are an item."

"I don't think so, Maggie." There he went again as if I had lost my mind or the idea was farfetched. He glanced around Vinnie's dash. "Damn, do you have the seat warmers on?" He asked with a perspiration on his top lip. "It's so hot, hens could lay hard-boiled eggs in here."

"No. I don't." I tapped the wheel knowing good and well it was Vinnie making Mick as uncomfortable as he could.

"Please let me get this car checked out for you. It's like a ticking time bomb." Mick lifted his hinny in the air.

I closed my eyes, anticipating Vinnie's reciprocation. And it came. Vinnie zoomed so fast over a pothole that it sent Mick's head into the roof, nearly breaking it off at the neck.

"Maggie," Mick rolled his head around his neck. "You about killed me. Slow down."

Vinnie took a sharp left on Magnolia before taking another quick left on Second and sliding up to the curb in front of The Derby. The cab was nowhere to be found and Vinnie was right. I needed a drink.

"The Derby?" Mick asked. "Now you want to drink?"

"Why not?" I acted as if I turned off the ignition. "I'm thirsty."

"While you drink, I'll ask you a few questions." Mick ran his hand over Vinnie's dash. "Starting with, how did your car show up on Fourth Street?"

Chapter Five

"Give me a seven-n-seven." I tapped on the bar when I got Buck's attention.

Lilith waved from the far end. I gestured toward her to let him know I'd be down there.

"Make it two." Mick held up two fingers and tapped his hand down the bar top until we reached Lilith.

Buck eyed Mick and then me. Under his knit cap, he was as bald as a cucumber and stout. He was a bartender here at the Derby and also a cage fighter. He's tried many times to get me and Lilith to come see him fight, but I found nothing interesting or appealing about seeing two men beat the crap out of each other in a closed cage.

"Hi, Mick." Lilith greeted Mick. "Where've y'all been?" She gave me a sly smile.

I rolled my eyes.

"I came downstairs from decorating and Auntie said Mick had come to steal you away. Lucky dog." Lilith curled her hands around her bourbon and ice and rested her forearms on the edge of the bar. "Mom is in rare form."

Buck put the two seven-n-sevens in front of us and Mick slid him some bills.

"If you girls need anything, let me know," Buck's words were meant for me and Lilith but his eyes focused on Mick.

"Do you and muscle man have a thing?" Mick asked me.

"No more than you and Miss Pumpkin Ginger." I picked up my glass and took a nice slow drink.

"You two sound like an old married couple instead of partners in crime." Lilith pulled her lips together and her eyes popped open.

"You told her that you work with me?" Mick let out a long deep sigh. "You know you weren't supposed to tell anyone. Including family."

"It's my sister. My best friend." I gave Lilith the wonky eye. She mouthed *sorry*.

"I'm going to the bathroom." He lifted his glass to his mouth and downed his drink.

I watched as he walked away. He lifted his hand at Buck and Buck nodded, knowing to fix Mick another round. Buck looked down at me and I wagged my hand. One was enough for me.

"I can't believe you just let it slip," I said. "It's not like I can wave my hand and poof he forgets. Remember, he is part of my Life's Journey and that little spell thing we've got going for us doesn't work on him."

"I swear I'm sorry. It's just that you two argue like you're a couple. And you'd make a cute couple." She wasn't telling me anything I didn't think already, but we were work partners and he made it clear that he wasn't interested when we were in the presence of Angela.

"We aren't," I groaned into my drink.

"Maggie, right?" A man walked up to me. "Brian Mingo. Gladys Hubbard's nephew from New York."

"Oh, yeah." I nodded before Lilith shoved past the front of me, pushing me further back on my stool.

"You say you're from New York? As in the city?" Lilith had always wanted to go to New York City but Mom refused to let her go. She said Lilith would lose her mind and put all sorts of spells on people. *She'd shelter the homeless*, Mom would say. *Find homes for the population of the dog pounds*, she'd follow up with when Lilith would protest.

Lilith did have a big heart and she did hate to see anyone down on their luck, animals included. That was probably why she had Gilbert. Big or small, she loved them all.

"I am. I'm here for the St. James Art Festival and my aunt was gracious enough to give me a place to stay."

"We've lived across from your aunt for so long, I'm surprised we've never met." Lilith patted the bar top next to her and Brian took his beer and sat down next to Lilith where they continued their conversation and she grilled him about NYC and how she'd love to do makeup there.

Mick came back and sat down next to me.

"Listen, Maggie." Mick leaned over his drink on the bar. "I'll let Burt know about someone following you. That way we can keep an eye out."

"I don't need anyone to keep an eye out for me." I ran my finger around the rim of the glass.

"At least let me see if I can get you a company car because your car isn't reliable." Mick had no idea what he was talking about and I appreciated the thought, but I was a little annoyed with him.

I couldn't determine if my feelings had anything to do with the fact that there were two women dead and he was the tie or the fact that he did seem to be a ladies man, which seemed to bother me more, especially with Angela Fritz.

"My car is just fine." I picked up the glass and took a couple of sips. Lilith got up and went toward the bathroom and I turned my attention to Brian. "You said you are in town for the St. James Art Festival?"

"I am. I'm actually here to see if there is any local talent I can showcase when I get back to NYC." He leaned his head around me and looked at Mick. "Brian Mingo." He stuck his hand across the bar and they clasped in front of me.

"Mick Jasper." Mick lifted his chin and gave a slight smile. "I saw you earlier at Maggie's neighbor's house. Big art guy from New York."

"Yes, my aunt." Brian rolled his eyes. "She has a tendency to exaggerate a little bit. She is very excited about the joint adventure she's got going with," he hesitated, "your aunt?"

"Ahh, yes." I lifted my glass and took another sip. "My auntie Meme and your aunt have a long standing history of arguing so when they decided to collaborate, needless to say I was a bit shocked."

Not really, but making mortal talk was so tedious. I really wanted to tell him that his aunt was nothing but nosy and we needed to get her out of her house so my mom could decorate our house the witchy way. A snap of the finger, but that obviously was a wasted day.

"I told her I'd stop by and check it out tomorrow." His glance grazed my shoulder as they followed Lilith back to the bar stool. "Would you like to dance?"

"Absolutely." Lilith didn't even have a chance to sit down before he grabbed her hand and dragged her to the dance floor in front of the jukebox as some old crooner sang a sad and slow country song.

Mick and I had rotated our stools to watch them. Brian seemed a little too close for comfort and I could feel Lilith pulling back from him. When they twirled and she was facing me, her stare told me it was about to get interesting.

Lilith was always getting hit on. That was how we came about playing Truth or Spell at The Derby.

"Ah, oh." Mick nodded his head toward Brian. "The old hand slide is a little too early."

Brian had decided it was a good idea to move his hand down Lilith's back to her rump. Clearly a wrong move because she slapped him right across the face before she jabbed his eye with her fist. I knew exactly what was coming next and I didn't need to play Truth or Spell to watch the show.

"It looks like there is going to be more than one family member in a feud with that family." I tried to talk to Mick before the puff of smoke appeared at the feet of what used to be the mortal two-legged human of Brian Mingo.

"Damn machine," Burt groaned from behind the bar. He lifted up the bar top on the end of the bar so he could get over to the jukebox.

"That's a fire hazard." Mick didn't take his eyes off of the smoke.

Only I knew it wasn't smoke from a faulty jukebox. It was a spell Lilith had put on Brian and the smoke was a wonderful cover up to explain where Brian had gone.

"I bet if you played better music it wouldn't do that." Lilith fanned her face on the way back to the stool and took her place as if nothing happened. When she tapped her toes on the floor and faced the bar top, the smoke cleared and everything was good.

"I swear this place is haunted," Burt growled after he had checked out the jukebox. "Nothing is wrong with that darn thing. It only does it when," Burt looked over at us, "you two are here." He cocked a brow.

"Oh and we did it?" I laughed and shook my head, knowing good and well we did it.

Mick and Burt talked about the crazy machine as I looked over my shoulder at the jukebox. The tiniest grey cat peeped its head around the jukebox. Its green eyes stared back.

"Meow," Lilith racked her fingers toward me.

"Where did Brian go?" Mick looked around. He pointed to the spot where Brian had been sitting. "He left his keys and a full drink."

He looked between Lilith and me. We both shrugged.

"I guess Lilith gave him the old one, two and scared him off." I picked up the drink to finish it off.

It'd been a long day and a long night. I had to still go over those files Burt had given me and get my opinion to him in the late morning. I'd already told Auntie Meme that I could help out in the diner in the morning and a late night wouldn't do me any good. I needed to be on my game if I was going to save Mick from being investigated. It hadn't been that long since I discovered my Life's Journey included Mick and I wasn't about to let this mess it up.

"He's a big boy. He will have to come back for his keys." I got up. "I've got a long day tomorrow." I jabbed Mick on his deltoid. "That includes saving your hide and going to supper with your ex-girlfriend."

"Whoa," Mick put his hands in the air after he threw a couple bills on the bar. "Angela Fritz isn't my ex-girlfriend."

I shot him the *yeah right* look.

"Not that we're an item." He stopped in front of me when I took a step forward. "Listen, Maggie." His eyes had a reserve that I couldn't place. "As much as you want to believe that I'm some Casanova, I'm not."

"It doesn't matter what I think." I walked around him and he followed me outside where Vinnie was waiting. "What matters is why these women are being murdered and you are the reason behind it."

He grabbed my forearm when I started to walk around the front of the car and dragged me closer to him.

"It does matter to me what you think." Mick's blue eyes and words seized my breath. Vinnie's horn tooted. He dropped his grip and looked at my insane familiar. "We are partners and partners are supposed to trust each other."

He left me speechless.

"Get the car fixed." He threw his hand in the air just as a cab drove by, causing the cab to skid to a stop. He disappeared into the back seat.

Chapter Six

"Say," I stood in the Jack and Jill bathroom between my and Lilith's rooms. She was getting ready for her big corporate job at Mystic Couture while I got ready to clean up after people at The Brew. "Do you have any Jockey Red that I can have?"

It was interesting how we both had completely different Life's Journeys.

"Don't you have some tubes?" She walked in the bathroom already dressed in her two-piece pink pant suit that made her dark features pop. Her black hair grazed the top of her shoulders and her blunt bangs hung perfectly over her dark eyes.

"I do, but I need a tube or two to give to Angela Fritz." I tugged my long black hair into a pony tail. I was a little envious of her cute outfit compared to my black skinny jeans, black tee, and black flats that were never seen under The Brew apron.

"Angela Fritz, the art person?" Lilith and I had no mortal culture what-so-ever.

"Yeah, you heard of her?" I asked as the curiosity tugged at me.

"She's supposed to come to the office this morning to get in some photos with some fall products because she's our new spokesperson for the line. She's crazy about Mystic Couture and doing a lot of press for us for the upcoming year." She looked in the mirror and ran her finger along the edges of her lips before she smoothed down her hair one last time.

"She invited me to supper at her hotel tonight and she was all over my lipstick. I thought it would be a nice gesture to take her a tube or two for inviting me." I leaned up against the bathroom door between the bathroom and her room and watched her put her sling-back black heels on.

"Sure. I have some in my bag or if you want you can come by the office after you leave the diner and I'll get a basket of goodies together." Lilith stood up.

"That's great." I would definitely get on Angela's good side, even though she really didn't want to invite me. I was just in the right place when she asked and she had too good of southern manners not to invite me.

Lilith and I headed downstairs just as there was a loud banging on the door.

"Can I help you?" I asked in a sarcastic tone when I flung the door open and nearly missed receiving the palm of Mrs. Hubbard on my face where the door had been. Her hair was spun tight around several pink sponge curlers all over her head. She had on her khaki pants and today she wore a white cardigan as her choice of color.

"Where is that sister of yours?" Mrs. Hubbard spat.

"She went to work." I pulled the door tight to my body so Lilith could slip by and head down the hall and out the back door to escape Mrs. Hubbard. "Aren't you coming to the diner this morning?"

"I am, but your sister did something to my Brian." She pointed to her house.

Brian Mingo was lying in the middle of the green between our houses. His clothes looked like they'd been clawed up and he was passed out.

"Why on Earth would you say that?" I asked.

"When I found him a minute ago, he was muttering Lilith's name and told me she was a tigress. Then he passed out again." She huffed and puffed. "My Brian is a high profile art dealer from New York City."

"Yeah, you told me." I glanced back over at Brian a little thankful that Lilith didn't put a full twenty-four hour spell on him because Mrs. Hubbard would've been going nuts looking for him.

"You have no regard for real jobs." Her eyes narrowed. "I want to talk to your mom."

"I'm sorry, Mom is still asleep and Auntie already left for The Brew." I noticed Auntie's bike was already missing from the front porch where she parked it every day after she got home from work.

She claimed it was good cardio exercise, but that didn't make much sense to me since the bike flew in the air like a broom. Granted, she pedaled it in the air, but not enough to get any exercise. It wasn't my place to argue with her. After all, she was a couple hundred years old.

"Something needs to be done about this." Mrs. Hubbard pointed to him just as Susie Brown and the group of other women who lived on Belgravia Court who loved to walk early in the morning nearly fell over each other looking at Brian lying on the grass among the leaves.

"Good morning, Gladys." Susie Brown walked in place but stood at the bottom of my porch with Shay Hannagan taking a much longer gander at Brian. The rest of the women continued to walk ahead. "What is your nephew doing in the middle of Belgravia Court with his clothes all ripped up?"

"Why do you think I'm over here this morning?" Mrs. Hubbard jutted a finger at me.

"I didn't do anything to him." I pulled my hand up to my chest.

"I told you Susie, there is something strange about this family." She looked over at Shay. "Stop looking at him."

"He looks drunk to me." Shay trotted over to us.

"He's not. He's a big art dealer. . ." her lips pursed when Susie Brown finished her sentence.

"From New York City. Yes, Gladys, you've told us a million times." Susie's brows cocked. "You left out the part where he is a drunk from New York City."

"Yes, I heard there are a lot of drunks and homeless people in New York City," Shay noted, keeping her eyes on Brian.

"He's not drunk or homeless!" Mrs. Hubbard's voice cracked as it escalated. She scurried back down the steps and gave Brian a nudge with her foot.

He rustled a little before she bent down and gave him an earful of something.

He stood up and stumbled over to her house and up her steps, but not without King taking a chunk out of his ankle.

Chapter Seven

"Good morning, Maggie." Vinnie greeted me when I got into the car. "Your mother put a bag of herbs on the seat that Meme is going to need for the daily specials. She said that you were sleeping when she finished making them and didn't want to disturb you."

"Thanks." I glanced over at the passenger seat. Instead of seeing herbs, I imagined Mick.

"Maggie, where is your mind this morning?" Vinnie asked and pulled out of the garage and down the alley.

"I can't help but think about Mick and if SKUL uncovered anything about those women." I watched as Vinnie's circuit went nuts, rolling red lights back and forth.

"I don't know what SKUL uncovered, but I came up with a list of women Agent Jasper has been associated with in more than a friendly manner." Vinnie's voice was static. "I must warn you that it's a pretty extensive list."

"Why would you warn me?" I asked brushing him off.

"Because I know you, Maggie Park and that heart of yours gets in the way every time." I hated it when Vinnie was right.

I was definitely attracted to Mick Jasper when I first met him at the diner before I'd even tried to put the spell on him that night at The Derby.

"We are partners. My Life's Journey." I knew Vinnie knew my words were my cover, but if I said them enough, my ear might help my brain to believe them.

"The women that have been murdered were in the same order as Mick had dated them. I'm wondering if you need to see the next woman on the list and warn her."

Vinnie had a good point. It couldn't hurt and it might give Burt a good lead to check into.

"Who is she and what is her address?" I asked and noticed Auntie's bike pulled up in front of the diner and the lights in the kitchen were burning bright behind the dark dining area.

"Angela Fritz." Vinnie's words stopped my heart.

"No," I said in astonishment. "He didn't date her."

"Oh, he did." Vinnie put up all sorts of photos of a younger Mick Jasper and a young, but still beautiful Angela Fritz at a couple of parties. "They became very chummy right before Agent Jasper had gone into the Army. They spent a couple of weeks together. In fact, Angela Fritz continued to mail Agent Jasper while he was overseas in Iraq."

"What happened to their relationship?" I didn't want to really know the answer but I knew I had to in order to figure out what was going on.

"Agent Jasper came back after his tour of duty and became part of Interpol and that's how he landed right back at home as an agent for SKUL." Vinnie shut off his engine. His circuit board shut down.

"You. . ." I waved my fist at him. He knew he'd given me a lot of information to chew on until I could do something about it.

I didn't know Mick Jasper at all. All I figured was that he was my Life's Journey and the rest would fall into place. Sure, I'd changed records of my history so SKUL could hire me as the civilian consultant, but I'd been completely relaxed on who I was actually working with.

"Good morning." I walked into the kitchen where Auntie Meme was standing in front of the stove watching the ladle go around and around in circles.

I gave her a quick kiss on the cheek.

"Is Gladys on her way?" Auntie Meme asked.

"I'm not sure. She's pretty mad at Lilith." I handed Auntie the baggie full of herbs Mom had left in Vinnie.

She took the bag.

"Fill up a couple of pots of water and stick them on the stove," she instructed me.

"What about the condiments?" I asked about the tables in the diner.

She clapped a couple of times above her head.

"Done." She went back to the herbs.

"But you don't let me use magic," I reminded her.

"Well, you don't have Gladys Hubbard standing over your shoulder while you try to cook either." She scooted her finger at me and the pots to hurry up.

I did what she told me to do and watched as she sprinkled some of the herbs in each pot. Instantly the water turned into delicious stacks of all different pancakes, bacon, sausage, the mini-cakes Mrs. Hubbard made, and many more different breakfast items.

While I took the orders and served the food, Auntie would look as if she were cooking more breakfast items, but really she'd be working on the lunch specials at that time.

I took the plated cakes into the diner and put them on the platter underneath the glass dome.

Mrs. Hubbard had her nose pressed up against the diner's front door with her hands over her eyes, looking in.

"Mrs. Hubbard is here," I said and walked to the door to let her in.

"You've already been busy." She harrumphed and waddled back to the kitchen.

There was a rumble of words between the two enemies. Mrs. Hubbard was mad that Auntie had already made the cakes and Auntie was fussing about how Mrs.

Hubbard was late. Mrs. Hubbard followed up with how she wouldn't have been late if it weren't for Lilith and her desire to snatch up the most eligible bachelor in New York City. Auntie said that Lilith wouldn't waste her gorgeous time on someone who liked to play with crayons.

It went back and forth until the first customer came into the diner.

"Have a seat anywhere," I yelled over my shoulder as I rolled up on my toes to turn on the TV that was hanging on the wall behind the counter.

Our regulars loved to watch TV and catch up on the news as they ate their food and drank their coffee.

"I'll have my regular," Joe Farmer said and eased onto his stool. He was sweet on Auntie Meme. "Don't forget to give me the aprons before I leave."

Joe was the owner of Farmer's Dry Cleaners down the street and he did all of The Brew's laundry for free since he was trying to score a date with Auntie. I've tried to persuade him to find other women, but he insisted Auntie would give in one day. So every day he was generally the first person at the diner and kept an eye on Auntie and if any man tried to compliment her on her cooking, Joe would eyeball them.

"Sherry." I was a bit shocked to see Sherry walking into the diner and not at SKUL.

The last time she'd been here, I'd taken her spot on the SKUL investigation team where she was to play the role of Mick's wife but someone on the bad side knew her from school. Needless to say, Burt had her work my shift at the diner while I worked at SKUL. Of course, Auntie put a spell on Sherry to be a good worker and not have to train her. But what was she doing here now?

"Can I get you something?" I asked as she took a stool at the counter at the opposite end of the counter from Joe.

"I'll take a coffee and have a talk with you." She glanced around. She had on her usual SKUL outfit. Blue trouser pants, gun in her holster, badge on her belt, and a white button down neatly tucked in.

Auntie stuck her head through the window. Joe straightened up on the stool in anticipation that Auntie would give him the time of day, but when she only addressed me, he slumped back down.

"What's she doing here?" Auntie asked with a critical tone.

"I don't know. Give me a couple biscuits and gravy, hold the spell," I warned Auntie Meme. I grabbed the coffee pot and moseyed over Sherry's way.

"Shucks," she grumbled and disappeared back into the kitchen.

That was how the food at The Brew worked. Auntie used magic to make the best food. She put a little spell into each order that left the customer full from not just filling their belly, but with a full heart of joy and happiness. That was her Life's Journey. To keep the citizens of Louisville happy and healthy. She claimed there was so much crime and sadness in the world that it was up to her to bring our part of the world a little peace. It seemed to work for her because we were always busy and most days had a wait list or line out the door.

"Here you go." I flipped over the white coffee cup in front of her and filled it to the brim. "What's up?" I asked and nodded at the customers walking in the diner so they knew I saw them.

"I've been thinking about Mick." Her hands curled around the steaming cup of coffee.

I leaned a hip up against the counter. "I'm listening."

"You and I only want what is best for him since we are his partners." She was right. "Maggie, he's in a lot of trouble. Burt sent me a message last night saying he believed the police were going to question Mick and might bring some sort of bogus charge against him to help ease the public's fear."

"What?" My jaw dropped.

"Yes. I think that maybe you and I should join forces, without Burt knowing of course, because he'd never go for it." She was right. Burt wouldn't want me poking my head around, even though I'd already planned to do so. "I'll see what I can dig up about the women."

She slipped a piece of paper across the counter. I picked it up and looked at it.

"What is Diggity Dog and these numbers?" I asked.

"That is my intelligence code and undercover name. Those will help you get into any system with any SKUL computers while you are at the office. It might help with something." She looked around again. "That's highly classified and Burt will fire me if he knows I gave that to you."

Auntie tapped the bell. I tucked the piece of paper in my apron and headed over to the window where Joe's breakfast was ready along with Sherry's biscuits and gravy. I grabbed Joe's plate and stuck it in front of him. I turned around and grabbed Sherry's, only to turn around to the dinging bell over the door and Sherry walking out.

Chapter Eight

"You mean she just gave you her code?" Vinnie asked on my way over to Mystic Couture to pick up that package from Lilith after I'd cleaned up The Brew after the lunch shift.

"Yes. I thought it was strange too," I said.

"That was easy." Vinnie knew I could've gotten the code myself if I'd gone to the office and did some witchy things, but this was way better.

I had the piece of paper in my hand and was looking at it as Vinnie zoomed down the street by the river, which was where Mystic Couture's manufacturing facility was located. I read off the code to Vinnie. He repeated them back to me so he made sure he could process the right information with the code.

"I'm going to go in here and get the package. You process that code." I got out of the car and headed into the guts of Mystic Couture's front office.

The chic office was exactly what you'd expect from a fancy company like Mystic Couture and Lilith fit right on in. There was red leather furniture and modern lighting all over the office. The desks weren't the normal wood, they were translucent and very modern. The designer hit the mark on the head with this cool design.

"Hi there, Maggie." The receptionist greeted me and immediately picked up the phone to call Lilith.

Within seconds, Lilith had come to the front with a huge basket of Mystic Couture products packaged together in cellophane. Her head peeked around the side of it so she could see where she was going.

"I hope you slam this in her face as soon as she opens the door." Lilith shoved the basket in my arms.

"Why? What happened?" I asked.

"After we'd gotten the best makeup artist in the world to fly here and do some sort of abstract makeup with the Mystic Couture line because *Angela Fritz*," Lilith said her name in a snooty way, "didn't want to show her real face, so she agreed to this abstract crap and then we got all the products she wanted, which isn't cheap. We hired the best photographer and the one she recommended all for a no show."

"No show?" I asked.

"Yeah. No. Show." Lilith turned on the balls of her feet and waved 'bye over her shoulder.

Angela seemed to be a lot of things, but she sure did seem to keep her commitments when it came to her job.

I said a quick goodbye to the receptionist and stuffed the basket into Vinnie's passenger side, which barely fit.

"We need to head straight to the Galt House," I said as soon as I got inside. "Angela Fritz was a no show."

"Maybe she had something to do," Vinnie said, starting his engine.

"Well, I'd like to know what that is. Plus, I'll give her this basket which will give me the in to ask her about Mick." I couldn't help but wonder why Mick had told me he hadn't dated her when clearly he had. "What did you find out about the codes?"

"Sherry is pretty good at her job. She takes it very seriously. Agent Jasper is her second partner. The first was killed while they were in the middle of an investigation. It took a toll on her and Agent Jasper stepped up to the plate to be her next partner." Vinnie read off her stats on solving the crimes and her personal stats on our way over to the Galt House.

The Galt House was the most popular hotel in Louisville. It was the official hotel of the Kentucky Derby and most celebrities that visited the area. Angela Fritz was no different.

The open glass dome interior with grey accents was a beautiful backdrop against the sunny, but chilly fall afternoon. There were guests milling around.

"Can I help you?" the concierge asked when he saw my big basket.

"I'm going to see Angela Fritz at the penthouse." I continued to walk.

"I'm sorry." He stopped me. Inwardly I groaned knowing I was going to have to use some magic. On him. "You are going to have to leave that with me."

"I've got it. I know Angela." I smiled and continued to walk.

"And your name?" He scurried next to me on my way to the elevator.

A big huff of air escaped me when I stopped at the elevator. I pulled the basket to the side of my body and blew a steady stream of air out of my mouth and into his face making him become very sleepy. His body slid down the wall and ended up on his butt with his head hung down.

I stepped into the elevator and stuck my finger next to my nose, sending the elevator up to the penthouse.

I put the basket on the floor next to my feet because it was heavy. I knocked on the door.

"Hi, Angela." I greeted her with a smile. "I'm Maggie, Mick's friend."

Her brown hair was down and flowed over her shoulder. Her eyes dull. She opened her mouth, "My art," she gasped and fell forward. I caught her in my arms.

"Angela?" I looked over her shoulder, down her back and couldn't help but see the knife sticking out of her back.

Chapter Nine

"Explain to me exactly why you are here?" Burt rubbed his bald head. By his expression, I could tell he wasn't one bit happy that I was there. We stood out in the hallway just a few feet from where I'd caught her. I had called Burt as soon as I dropped her on the ground, which wasn't as graceful as I wished I'd done, but I'd never caught a nearly dead person that then died in my life.

There was a flurry of people that included police, SKUL agents, hotel employees, and emergency staff milling around the room. The police were keeping everyone away from some sort of evidence they were collecting and the SKUL agents were questioning the hotel staff. There was something said about the security camera, which I'd love to get my hands on. The EMTs were still hovered over Angela Fritz's body that was still half in the hall and half in the hotel room.

"I met Angela Fritz yesterday when Mick and I went to the St. James Art Festival. She and Mick have been long-time friends." My lips twitched, keeping the secret inside of me that Mick and Angela did have a fling. It was something I wanted to take up with him when we were not around so many eyes. "She knew my lipstick color, which happens to be from Mystic Couture, which was my first case with SKUL," I reminded him.

"Yes." Burt continued to rub his head and looked at his shoes. "Keep going."

"I told my sister about it and she said that Angela Fritz had agreed to be their new spokesperson for their new makeup line." My words caused Burt to jerk up and look at me.

"She doesn't like her picture taken," he said and pulled me out of the way when the EMT nearly knocked us down taking Angela Fritz's body down the hall to the elevator.

"You're right." I nodded. "Her contract had Mystic Couture bring in an abstract makeup artist that would use the Mystic Couture makeup to disguise her look. It was a very expensive campaign. Only Angela Fritz didn't show up." I cocked a brow.

"And you know that how?" Burt asked.

"Oh, yeah." I had to backtrack. "I was going to get some lipstick as a thank you gift for inviting me to supper today for Angela."

Burt's head tilted to the side, his eyes narrowed. He was confused.

"Angela had invited me, Mick, and Big Stevenson to supper tonight at her hotel before she leaves town tomorrow." Clearly she'd already left town. . .the dead way. I shook my head. "So I went to Mystic Couture to pick up the lipstick. That's when my sister told me about her not showing up for the photo shoot and literally shoved this basket of goodies at me that Angela was going to get at the shoot."

"So you decided to come on by and give it to her instead of waiting until tonight?" Burt asked.

"I got excited about the makeup package," I lied. I really wanted to ask her about Mick—I didn't think she'd be the next victim.

"Sir," Sherry popped her head out of the room. "Can I see you for a second?"

"Sure." Burt walked into the room and I followed.

The fall sun was fading fast as the afternoon drew to a close and the penthouse had an amazing view from the windows. I walked over and looked out over the river. The noise from below caught my attention. I looked down where the news and reporters had collected in front of the hotel. They were taking photos, holding microphones out, and screaming for attention as the EMTs wheeled Angela out to the ambulance.

The hat. My heart dropped.

The person with the hat that I'd seen a couple of times now was standing at the back of the group of rubber-neckers that were trying to see what was going on. Slowly the hat tipped up the side of the building and up to the penthouse windows.

I gulped as my insides churned and my necklace warmed against my chest.

The last of the burnt sunshine cast the shadow of the hat's brim down on the face. The only feature I could see was the pointy chin before the mystery hatted person disappeared into the walking crowd.

"Are you okay?" Sherry came up behind me.

"I'm fine." I shook off the feeling I'd gotten from the hatted mystery person. I dropped my hand from my necklace. It was no longer hot to my chest, which told me that the person with the hat was someone who needed to be found. "I just can't believe this."

"Are you thinking what I'm thinking?" she asked.

"I don't want to be thinking it, but I do believe that someone is trying to frame Mick." My eyes slid past her shoulder just as Mick hurried through the door.

"Maggie?" Mick's face melted when he saw me. He rushed over and touched my arm.

"Mick, I'm so glad to see you." I dragged him to me. "She had a knife stuck in her back."

"I know." Mick lips pursed. "She shouldn't have. . ."

"No!" The loud scream caused both of us to turn and look at the brunette woman I'd seen yesterday at the art festival. Her hollow eyes slid toward Mick and me. She sucked in a deep breath and her face stilled along with her glare at Mick. Sherry rushed over to her.

She and Burt led the woman to the couch where she buried her head into her hands and sobbed. The police officer came over and took over for Burt and Sherry.

Mick and I stood there trying to take it all in before she said something to Burt that caused him to walk over.

"Mick," Burt walked up with an unexpected concerned look on his face. "I'm going to have to ask you to take a leave of absence."

"Why?" Mick asked. I felt his anger as much as I saw it on his face.

"This is the third woman this week that has died and the only link to each other is you." He held up a piece of paper with Mick's address and phone number along with Angela Fritz's cell phone where there was a recent photo taken of them.

Mick ran his hand through his hair and let out a long sigh.

"I can explain that." He pointed to the evidence the police decided to come over and bag.

"No need to say anything until you meet with the SKUL lawyer and the SKUL psychiatrist." Burt pointed to the door. "I think it's best you leave and wait until you hear from me."

"Psychiatrist?" Mick questioned. "I didn't do this."

"I'm not saying you did, but someone sure does want us to think you did." Burt's words curled around my neck like a noose.

Chapter Ten

"Vinnie, I need you to tell me everything about the staff that Angela Fritz had," I said to Vinnie.

After Burt had released me, they kept Mick for more questioning and it was disheartening watching him turn his badge over to Burt. Sherry and I looked at each other as if we knew what we needed to do.

"Can you also text Sherry the list of Mick's women along with their addresses. We want to check them all out and at the very least make sure they are alive." I had to put the photo I'd seen of Mick and Angela in the back of my head.

I'd noticed Mick had on the same clothes as in the photo.

"Wait!" I yelled at Vinnie to stop. "Can you pull up close to the Galt House security room and get me a look at the security camera?"

"Maggie, you and I both know that the police are already all over the system." Vinnie was good at how things worked in the familiar world, but not so great in the mortal world.

"Yes, I bet you are right. Only they have to get a warrant to gain access and then view it." I ran my hand along his dashboard. "They don't have a Vinnie."

"And this is why your Life's Journey is to work with SKUL." Vinnie's engine roared and his tires squealed as he did a U-turn in the middle of the road.

He pulled up to the service entrance of the hotel next to the dumpster.

"It sure does smell here. I hope the stink doesn't peel my paint job." Vinnie's engine shut off. His circuit board rolled red.

"Oh, look at you trying to make a joke," I chuckled.

It was rare for Vinnie not to be serious about everything when it came to me. Maybe he was getting a little more of a social side.

"I took the video camera from the elevator up to the penthouse and the footage from the hallway looking down to the penthouse door along with the front entrance." Vinnie's circuit board turned into a grainy movie screen. "The entrance doesn't show Agent Jasper coming or going. Though it does show him in the elevator going up to the penthouse. Once he exits the elevator, you can see him get off and walk to the penthouse door where Angela Fritz steps outside to talk to him. There seems to be a bit of an argument between them," Vinnie did a play-by-play.

"Roll it back and zoom in on them." I watched as Mick's and Angela's actions went backward in slow motion.

When Vinnie played the footage again, I noticed Angela was crying. Mick at one point tried to touch her but she jerked away. Vinnie continued to play the video. Angela didn't let him in. She shut the door. He stood there for a couple of minutes before finally going back into the elevator.

"If he didn't go out of the front doors, where did he enter and exit the hotel?" I asked Vinnie.

"Good question. I can see there are no cameras in the kitchen but other than that, it's all I know." Vinnie's circuit rolled red.

"Okay." I wasn't sure what I was going to do with this information. I had to figure something out quick because the police would get the warrant and Mick would definitely be arrested for Angela Fritz's death. "Was Mick the last person to visit Angela?"

"It appears that way on the video. Also it shows you on the video going up the elevator." Vinnie played the footage. It clearly played me talking to the concierge and then he suddenly fell asleep. "I am most certain that we need to erase that."

"I agree." I was lucky to have him looking out for me. The last thing the police needed to see was me talking to the concierge and not having clearance to go to the penthouse, much less the unexplained sleeping episode of him.

Vinnie pulled out from behind the dumpster and headed toward home.

"Mick said something very strange to me." I bit my lip. "He said 'she shouldn't have'."

"Shouldn't have what, Maggie?" Vinnie asked.

"I don't know. That's when the brunette woman came into the room." The images of the person in the hat kept coming into my head. "When my necklace warmed, you knew I had seen that person in the hat again."

"Yes. I tried to follow but lost the person down an alleyway before I could get a full body scan to tell me if the person under the hat and black coat was a female or male," frustration was held in Vinnie's voice.

"Not only has that person come to the diner and the art festival, they were now also at the hotel where they knew I was or where they killed Angela." I looked out the window as Vinnie got on the interstate heading toward Old Louisville.

I was going from one fire to a frying pan. Who knew what was happening on Belgravia Court? I wondered if Susie Brown and Shay Hannagan had Mrs. Hubbard up in arms because I could guarantee the two women had already spread the news about Brian's indelicate state to the rest of the gossip-loving women of Belgravia Court.

"Maggie," Vinnie's voice was stressed. "I think we are being followed. Hold on."

Vinnie's engine picked up speed and roared underneath my feet. I turned around in my seat to see the car. I knew with pulse-pounding certainty the car was following us.

"Hold on, Maggie." Vinnie took the next exit nearly jumping the curb.

My stomach clenched tight as did my eyes when I saw Vinnie swerve into a line of traffic, barely avoiding a collision with another car. Panic rioted within me as the trailing car inched closer and we were stuck in traffic.

"This wasn't very bright," I said and jumped out of Vinnie when he came to a stop. There was only one way to figure out who was following me and that was to confront the person.

I brought my hand to my necklace and said a protection spell as I drew an X with my finger across my heart. The black car had tinted windows and my hand shook as fearful images of who was inside built up in my mind before I jerked the door handle.

"It's you," My voice broke with uncertainty as to why the brunette woman I'd seen with Angela at the art festival and at the hotel would be following me. "Get out." I pointed my finger at her sorrowful eyes.

"I needed to know where you were going," she spoke in a soft voice. "I have to know who killed her."

She dropped her hands from the steering wheel and into her lap. Her head bobbled as sobs escaped her lips. Her sadness struck a chord in my heart that I knew I should ignore. But I couldn't.

"Fine. You can follow me to a little diner I know and we can talk." I knew it was well after closing time at The Brew and Auntie Meme would be long gone. It would be the perfect place for me and this woman to talk. "What is your name?"

"Georgette Treminski. I've been Angela Fritz's assistant for over six years. There are a lot of things I know that may help out." She nodded as she made a decision. "I'll follow you."

The beeping horns of the irritated drivers didn't bother me any. I had a murder, well three murders, now to solve and hopefully Georgette Treminski had an answer I could work with.

Vinnie pulled up to the curb of The Brew. It wasn't like we needed a key to the front door. We simply touched it with our fingers, but for times when people were with us, we had dummy keys made for show.

Like my key fob for Vinnie. I pushed the button and Vinnie did the beeping even though the fob wasn't hooked up. I reached into the glove box for my set of dummy keys.

"You stay here and keep watch," I instructed Vinnie before pulling my sweater from the floor board.

As soon as the sun went down in the autumn, the chill in the air was almost too much to bear without a coat. At least for me.

Georgette had parked her car right behind Vinnie and she met me at the door. She had nice brunette hair with natural highlights. The kind of natural highlights that sent a woman's heart and soul into an itch of envy that no matter how much you tried to scratch it, you just couldn't. She had small hazel eyes with an average frame. She wasn't too skinny or too big. Just normal. She definitely wasn't as pretty at Angela, which I was positive why Angela hired Georgette, so as not to be out done.

I jimmied my fake key into the front door of The Brew and tapped the outside of the lock with the pad of my finger. The door opened and the lights flipped on.

The dining area had been left exactly as it should've been. The salt and pepper shakers along with the rest of the condiments needed to be refilled for the next day, which was something I'd do in the morning.

"Would you like a cup of coffee?" I asked Georgette as I walked back behind the counter to the coffee pot. All I had to do was pretend to flip the switch, then the perfect idea popped into my head. Georgette was not my Life's Journey so a little truth spell could potentially help me break the ice and not have to try so hard to get answers out of her.

"I'd like that." There was a thin smile on her lips that dipped down on the edges.

"Have a seat." I gestured to the stool in front of me on the other side of the counter. "I need to grab something from the kitchen."

I disappeared into the kitchen to find the herb that Mom used for the truth spells Auntie Meme put in some recipes. *Sometimes the best thing for a full stomach, besides my biscuits, is a dose of the truth,* Auntie would say when she knew that someone was in the diner for emotional eating because they either couldn't take the truth about something or tell the truth about something.

"Where is it?" I looked in the cabinet space around the kitchen until I found it in the jar labeled flour. Don't ask me why Auntie Meme would put it there because I had no idea. "The coffee should be about. . ." I pushed myself with my rear through the swinging door between the kitchen and the diner. "Auntie Meme." My jaw dropped as she and her Spell Circle stood in the middle of The Brew in their full regalia including their flying brooms.

She was stroking a little brown bunny that nestled in her arms.

"Ah, oh." Pixie's mouth formed an 'O'. She stood four feet tall by four feet wide and had a buzz cut. She looked between Auntie Meme and me.

I glanced around the room.

"Where is the girl that was sitting there?" I pointed to the stool where Georgette used to be.

"Who?" Auntie's brows lifted as her voice escalated.

"You know who," my voice husky as I stalked over to her. I pointed at the bunny. "Is that her?"

"Well. . ." Auntie's jaw tensed. "Miss Kitty interrupted our Spell Circle and told me that someone was sitting at the counter here," she referred to her owl that was her familiar. "The girls," she waved her hand in front of Pixie, Flora, Charmary, and Glinda, "and I decided we better fly on over and see what was going on."

"You turned her into a bunny?" Anger started to boil in me.

"I didn't see you in there until it was too late." Glinda stepped up to take the blame. The button on her cape was about to pop off due to her middle age spread. She had sweet eyes that almost got lost behind her straight hair that was parted down the middle and hung to her shoulders. "My grandchildren have always wanted a bunny and I just figured. . ."

I gave her the stink eye and grabbed Georgette out of Auntie Meme's arms.

"She is a very important witness for my Life's Journey with SKUL. I needed to talk to her. Didn't you see Vinnie outside?" I asked and glanced past the women in the Spell Circle.

He was gone.

"Damn, familiar. Where is he when I need him?" I grumbled and tried to hold the bouncy bunny securely in my arms. "Now what am I going to do?"

I looked between the women who were supposed to be elders of our community who should be teaching younger witches the proper ways to behave and interact with mortals. All of them looked confused and dumfounded.

"Well?" I stared directly at each one waiting for an answer. "Well," I sighed. "I guess I'm on my own."

The tap at the window caught our attention.

"Could this night get any worse?" I asked when we noticed it was Mick Jasper tapping on the door. "Don't say a word about this." I held the bunny up to them as I walked backward toward the door. "What are you doing here?" I asked Mick when I opened the door.

"Taking a walk." He peeked around me before his eyes settled on the bunny. "New friend?"

"Something like that." I sucked in a deep breath.

"That coffee smells good." Mick walked past me. "What good book are we reading this month?"

"*Tale of Five Witches*," Charmary spoke up. She was as thin as a cake of soap and six feet tall. Her grey hair made her look older than she was.

"Hhmmm." Mick eased down on the stool that had been recently occupied by Georgette. "I don't think I know that one."

"It's a good one." Flora cackled. Her five-foot-five-inch frame bounced up and down as she was so proud of her answer.

"It's not that good," I answered in a sarcastic tone.

"Book club is over." Auntie Meme held her broom, brush side up.

The Spell Circle got into a circle and lifted their brooms in their right hands, getting ready to knock the sticks on the black and white tiles to transport them back to wherever it was they had been meeting.

"Ahem," I cleared my throat. Mick looked at me and watched as I walked around the counter to get the coffee. "I couldn't decide what to do after I left the hotel so I came on down here and made some coffee to go over some clues."

I kept his attention as the Spell Circle disappeared.

"You like it black right?" I asked and set the bunny on the counter.

"I'm sure the board of health wouldn't approve of this." He pointed to the bunny and dragged the cup of coffee toward him.

"Watch the bunny." I headed to the kitchen to look for a box and when I didn't see one, I snapped one right into my hands, along with some bunny food and bedding.

"Where did that come from?" Mick asked when I stuck the box on the counter and placed the bunny in it. "Where did the book club go?"

"I brought this with me and was getting it ready in the back before you came in. The Spell. . ." I swallowed and picked up my cup of coffee, "The book club left out the door."

I looked at the door and noticed Vinnie was back. My eyes narrowed as my mind wondered where he'd been. Did he see the person in the hat again?

"Now, you need to tell me what you meant when you said 'she shouldn't have' before Georgette came into Angela's room." I wasn't going to let him leave until I had some sort of answers.

After he hesitated and continued to drink his coffee, I finally said, "I'm your only hope at this point."

His chest heaved up and down. He bit the corner of his inner lip as it looked like he was contemplating telling me something.

"Spill it. I've got all the time in the world and the coffee to go with it." I grabbed the pot and refilled our cups. "Why don't you start as far back as your time in the Army?"

"How did you know that?" he asked. "All of my information is confidential."

"Burt hired me for a reason and it wasn't just for my good looks," I joked. "But I'm going to have to say that this killer is going to keep going until they're stopped."

"What does that have to do with my past?" He continued to resist telling me what I wanted to hear.

"Because this is personal about you and I'm trying to help get your badge back." I picked up my mug and took a sip.

"I don't know how my history is going to help, but here it goes." Mick looked off into the distance. "I went straight into the Army ten years ago, the day I graduated from high school."

He continued to stare off, his voice monotone.

"There was nothing good about going to Iraq. There was gunshots, IEDs, death. That was it. I'd let not only myself down, but also I let a very good friend die. I knew after my tours were over that I still needed to help keep crime down, but decided to become a member of SKUL after they'd given me the psychiatric evaluation." He shook his head. "As a matter of fact, I had my first appointment with the SKUL psychiatrist Burt set me up with this afternoon. He gave me that same quiz. It brought back so many memories."

"I know this is hard." I placed a hand on top of his. Our eyes met. I felt an eager affection coming from him. There was no way he was guilty of these murders. "But you might say something to uncover something or someone that might be trying to get even with you after all of these years."

"God, Maggie." He dragged his hand from under mine and stood up. "Years and years of solving crimes. There could be multiple people who want to kill me."

"But that someone has to know who you really are because when we work a case, we are mostly undercover." This was how I knew this was more personal than professional. "Why did you go to the hotel to see Angela today?"

"How did you know that?" he asked.

"I have my ways. And it won't be long until the police get the warrant for the security cameras," I warned.

"Fine." He paced back and forth across the diner floor. "Angela called me last night. She asked me to come have a glass of wine. She wanted me to slip up the back because she didn't want anyone to see me or think we were an item. She's a private person like that." He paused. He smiled. "Anyways, she said that she was being stalked by a man that claimed she stole his ideas. She asked me to investigate. I went back to the office and did a little digging around. The particular painting she claimed the man said was his own, was in fact his."

He pulled a piece of paper out of his pants pocket. He handed it to me.

"Franklin Bingo. The artist. I contacted him and he told me she lifted the painting and claimed it as hers." He sighed.

"*The Ville*?" I asked.

"Yep." He confirmed my suspicion. "And I went back to tell her that I'd confirmed it through multiple sources— Mr. Bingo's sources along with the original painting—she had a meltdown. She got angry. Said that if I let this become public that she'd be finished. She confessed that she didn't paint it, her assistant, Georgette Treminski had in fact painted it. When the art agent came to see Angela, she fell in love with *The Ville* and sold it for millions of dollars." He glanced at me. "Now Georgette is missing."

"Really?" I drew my eyes to the bunny in the box.

"Yeah. Now they are looking into her for killing Angela and making this a completely unrelated case to me." He stopped pacing. "That puts us back to square one."

I wanted to scream that he was wrong. There was no way that Georgette did it or skipped town. I ran my hand down the fur of the big brown-eyed rabbit and wondered just how long it was going to be until this spell ran its course. This little bunny had some secrets and she'd been about to tell me everything before Auntie Meme and her Spell Circle ruined it.

Chapter Eleven

"Whose big idea was it to turn Georgette into a bunny?" I asked when I stepped through the kitchen door with the Georgette and her box underneath my arm.

Auntie Meme and her Spell Circle were sitting around the kitchen table with Mom. They'd exchanged their witch hats for Santa hats. The kitchen didn't look any different from when I'd left earlier this morning. And it was the only room Mom was in charge of.

"We don't have time to worry about some bunny." Auntie laughed as though she'd just made a joke. "Your mother is having a crisis."

"Crisis?" I asked and set the bunny and her box on the ground.

Riule crept over and looked into the box. The bunny backed itself up in the corner of the box.

"Riule, not for you," Mom scolded. He growled at Georgette before he jumped up into Mom's lap.

"What's your crisis, Mom?" I asked and sat down in the chair next to her.

"I'm broken." Her lips thinned with displeasure. "I can't seem to decorate or call up an inkling of creativity unless it's for Halloween."

"You mean you don't have creativeness like mortals do? And that you can't decorate unless you snap your fingers?" I asked.

"Yes. That's exactly it." She planted her elbows on the kitchen table and rested her chin in her hands. "I looked at your tree and the decorations you did in the snowman room."

"You mean the family room?" I asked.

"Yes. Then I saw the entrance and what your auntie did with the winter wonderland theme." Mom was right. Auntie Meme's entryway was magical.

She'd replaced the bright white light bulbs with icy blue ones and draped tiny strings of blue lights all over the ceiling. The Christmas trees she used had white frosted tips and crystal snowflakes hanging down from the branches. There were big presents wrapped in silver and white wrapping paper that sparkled with glitter and made you feel like you were in the best place on Earth.

"And you think that we did that in the little time we were here the mortal way?" I asked.

Auntie Meme sat in the chair next to Mom, but Mom's back was to her. She dragged her finger across her throat and her eyes widened, telling me to hush.

Mom jerked around when she noticed I was looking over her shoulder. Auntie Meme cleared her throat and straightened up in the chair as she curled her hand around a cup of special brew they made just for the Spell Circle.

"Auntie?" Mom eyed her. There was no way she could deny the evidence.

"Mom, really? You think that we have the gene in our body to just decorate for Christmas?" I wiggled my finger above my head. My pointy hat appeared and floated above my head. I dragged my finger in a downward motion to rest it on my head. "We are witches. We love black cats, pumpkins, cauldrons, cobwebs, spiders and all things mortals associate with Halloween."

"Maggie, I know our heritage," she retorted in cold sarcasm. "We live among the mortals and you know that I want to fit in just as much as Mrs. Hubbard."

"You think that old bat fits in?" Auntie cackled. "Well, if you stop this nonsense about not decorating our way, I don't have to put up with her nonsense at The Brew."

"We could give our little bunny friend a friend." Charmary lifted her brows up and down mischievously.

"No!" I stuck my hand out. "No more bunnies."

All of us looked over at the box. Riule still had his eyes on the frightened little bunny.

"Don't tell me." Mom planted her head in her hands and shook it back and forth. "Is that a mortal?"

"Yes. A mortal that is vital to my Life's Journey," I growled. "They turned her into a bunny."

"Miss Kitty told me someone was in the diner and we showed up." Auntie always felt like she could justify using magic on mortals. "It's not like she's going to remember."

"She might not remember, but I need her right now. Not in a few hours when she comes to." There was a faint twinkle in the depths of Charmary's eyes. "What?" I asked when the Spell Circle started to fidget in their seats.

"I need to get going, Meme." Pixie stood up and waddled to the door. "Good to see you, Fae," she addressed my mother and didn't look at me.

There was an uncertainty that aroused in me.

"Shoowee, look at the time." Flora looked at her naked wrist as if she were reading the time. "I've got to get my broom serviced in the morning."

Charmary lifted her gangly arms in the air and let out a big yawn. "It's almost my bed time." She stood up.

The three of them stood at the door and stared at Glinda. Pixie's eyes opened wide and she gave Glinda a slight nod.

"Oh yeah," Glinda pushed herself up to standing. "It's late."

"Oh, no." I jumped up and ran over to the door to block them from exiting, though they probably weren't going to use the door. "Is something going on here?"

Collectively the four of them shook their heads and mouthed no. Their foreheads wrinkled. Auntie Meme got up and walked over.

"Okay, girls. I'll see you next week." She started to push them out the door.

"Wait!" I yelled. "When I mentioned the spell on Georgette, you all got jittery."

Each of them looked in a different direction.

"Are you telling me that the spell you put on her is not going to wear off in a few hours?" My eyes narrowed more and more as I took turns looking at each of them.

My annoyance with them took over my body, my hands started to shake.

"Calm down, Maggie." Auntie put her hand on my arm. I jerked it away.

"What is wrong with you witches?" I sucked in a deep breath. "She was just sitting on a stool at the counter."

"I understand that, but when we didn't see anyone we knew, we thought she was robbing the place." Charmary tried to explain why they did such a deep spell.

"Did she look like she was a criminal?" I asked.

"Well, no." Pixie shrugged. When Glinda nudged her with her elbow, Pixie changed her stance. "I mean you never can be so sure. I mean, she was trespassing."

"She was with me." I pointed to myself and then drew my finger toward Georgette. "Now, undo it."

"We can't just undo it." Auntie straightened herself with dignity.

"You better get in your little circle." I gestured a circle with my finger. "And figure it out."

"Oh, dear." Glinda wrung her hands. "Oh, dear."

"It's not really that simple." Mom stood up and walked over to the box. She bent down and picked up the bunny. She looked it in the eyes. "When you undo a spell that doesn't have a time restraint, you are altering the recipient's already altered destiny that'd been forced on them."

"I don't care about her destiny. I care about what she was going to tell me before these five decided to create a spell where no spell was needed," I spat. "I'd be ashamed," I scolded them.

They looked between each other.

"What?" They had some sort of secret between them. I could feel it. "Tell me."

"One of us could reverse the spell, but it puts us on probation for the next three months," Pixie said.

"Pixie," Charmary groaned. "Hush."

"Yeah, hush." Glinda's face scrunched in disapproval.

"It should be Glinda." Flora pointed to Glinda. "She's the one who did it because her grandchildren want a bunny."

"Yep, Glinda should be the one." Charmary folded her arms as she sold out her friend. "Right Meme?"

"As right as rain." Auntie Meme dragged her chin up and down in a dramatic way. "Yep." She pointed to Glinda. "Her."

"Well, I never," Glinda cried out. "Each of you were chanting for me to do it. We'd have never been in the situation if it weren't for you." She jutted her finger at Auntie.

"I'm two hundred years old and half crazy. Since when have any of you listened to me?" she asked.

Mom and I sat back and enjoyed the show as the Spell Circle was falling apart.

"What are you talking about?" Pixie's nose curled. "We always listen to you."

"Yeah, so you should be the one to go on probation," Glinda suggested.

"Um," I started to speak up for Auntie Meme, but Mom stopped me. She lifted her finger to her lips, winked and shook her head.

"Let them sort this out," she leaned over and whispered. "This is all their fault."

Then an all-out war started between the women. Sparks were flying in the air as they flung their hands around. Georgette backed up in the box corner and even Riule darted out of the room. Mom simply sat with a smile on her face, legs crossed and swinging slowly.

"What about you? You are the one who said that we needed to stop our meeting when Miss Kitty showed up even after I said it could wait." Auntie looked at Charmary.

"Me? It was your diner that was getting broken into." Her gangly features squished up on her face.

A rush of wind swirled around us in a small tornado pattern settling into a puff of glitter with Lilith standing in the middle.

"That was an entrance." Flora stuck her hand on her hips.

"I knocked on the door so I didn't hit you, but y'all were too busy fussing with each other to even notice." Lilith tucked a strand of her hair behind her ear. "A bunny!" She squealed and walked over to Mom where Georgette was shaking with deep-set fear.

"No, that's Georgette Treminski. Long story short." My finger dragged in front of the Spell Circle women. "I had taken Georgette to the diner for coffee and Miss Kitty told them someone had broken into the diner. They showed up while I was in the kitchen and turned her into a bunny with no spell end time."

"And according to the old witchy ways, whoever did the spell can't undo it unless they go on probation which means no. . ." Lilith wiggled her fingers in the air.

"Bummer." The edge of her lip cocked as she gave a sympathetic look at Georgette.

Lilith was always so much better than me about the history of the witches. She always studied and read all the material when we were in witch school while I'd wanted to have sleepovers and friends the mortal way. Witch school was at night after we'd gone to a full day at mortal school. Lilith pretty much slept through mortal school, whereas I was eager. The reverse for witch school.

"You do know about that new invention for spell reversal if it's within the first three hours." Lilith might've just saved Georgette.

"Then we better hurry up!" Flora looked down at her bare wrist.

"How long has it been?" Mom asked as she got up and put the bunny back in the box.

"They've wasted at least an hour here, trying to put the blame on each other." I grabbed the box and headed to the basement door.

"Young lady!" Mom's voice stopped me. "What do you think you are doing? There are some traditions that aren't updated or have new inventions."

"Fine." I set the box down and ran my hand up and down my body. The others followed before the chant started.

"Boom, cha, ka, la, ka. Boom, cha, ka, la, ka." Auntie Meme, Mom, Lilith, and the Spell Circle chanted after donning the traditional pointy hats on top of their heads. "Boom, cha, ka, la, ka. Boom, cha, ka, la, ka." Auntie Meme and Lilith had gotten into a good groove and I joined them.

The black cloak was tied tightly around my neck as the sides flew behind me when I picked Georgette's box back up. The basement door opened. The twinkling lights on the ceiling and railing illuminated the way with each step we took into the darkness. At the end of the steps, the cobblestone hallway was too narrow for all of us to walk side-by-side. We formed a single-file line with me leading the way with the box in my hand.

"Boom, cha, ka, la, ka. Boom, cha, ka, la, ka." The chant level lowered to a whisper as we walked deeper and deeper into the depths of the basement. The twinkling lights were long gone and gas-lit lanterns hung on the wall to light the rest of the way.

Where the cobblestone stopped, there was a big, heavy wooden door with a circular stained-glass window that took up most of the center of the door. The stained glass held three stars that represented the Coven crest.

I tucked the box under my arm and used my other hand to tap on each star.

"The first star represents family. The second star represents honor to the Coven. The third star represents honor to thyself." It was part of the ritual that had to be performed before you could go into the sacred room.

I fisted my hand and placed it above the black hardware giving two-short knocks and dragged my knuckles down the wood for one long knock. The door swept open on its own and opened up into the red room where the one hundred candles burned from the large gold chandelier that hung in the center of the room. Little puffs of smoke dotting off the wicks of the candles. The Coven crest was also on a rug that was strategically placed in the middle of the room. A large black cauldron sat in the middle of the rug.

Lilith's cape swung around and curled around her body. The only part of her that was showing was her face. The candles illuminated her olive skin, casting a mysterious shadow down her face.

She motioned for me to bring the box with the bunny in it to the center of the room. The low chant behind me stayed low but picked up speed. I put the box down where Lilith had pointed and took a step back in place.

The chant continued as Lilith picked up Georgette and plucked a few of her hairs, tossing them into the bubbling cauldron. She held the bunny over the cauldron and tapped each one of the bunny's toenails, clipping them, letting them fall into the cauldron, sending the frothy mix in a swirling motion.

She placed the bunny back in the box and raised her arms in the air. The cape swung behind her shoulders. She plucked a strand of her own hair, making it strong and straight like a stick. She stirred the cauldron three times and said, "Bound ye thee, unbound ye thou. Keep your memory away, now go."

She lifted the stick into the air and held it over the bunny in the box. The residue of the mix on the stick dripped down the stick and like a tear, it dropped down into the box.

A screech escaped the bunny. Lilith stepped back and we all watched with anticipation at what was going to happen. We didn't have to wait long because soon after the bunny screeched, it started to take on the form of a human and before long, Georgette was back to her mortal self.

"Veruck!" Lilith threw her finger at Georgette.

In an instant, Georgette was gone.

Chapter Twelve

"Don't let her in!" Auntie Meme yelled through the pass through of the kitchen window into the diner.

"I'm going to let her in." I started to walk toward the front door. It was way too early to listen to anyone fight and fuss. "After what you put me through last night, I'm exhausted."

"You and I both know that your mother isn't at home working on those decorations. And this morning, like you, I'm in no mood to listen to Gladys Hubbard." Auntie shook a finger at me.

"Good morning, Mrs. Hubbard." I flung the door open wide.

"Good morning? Good morning?" She scoffed and walked past me into the kitchen. "It's not been a good morning. I'm still the butt of all the gossip on Belgravia Court."

I grabbed the container caddy from underneath the counter and started on the left side of the diner.

"I'm not going to do it!" Mrs. Hubbard yelled right before the sound of pots smacking against each other echoed out of the kitchen and into the dining room.

"Then I'm boycotting and you can do this all on your own!" The swinging door between the kitchen and the dining room swung open, smacking the wall. Auntie Meme stomped out. Her cheeks redder than normal along with a quicker step. "I'm done!"

Auntie Meme plopped down on a stool. Her upper lip flinched.

"Coffee?" I picked up the coffee pot and flipped over the white cup in front of her before she could answer me.

There was no time to refill the condiments on the table. I snapped my wrist and the tables and diner were ready for the morning rush.

I poured myself a cup of coffee and sat down next to Auntie Meme.

"This is good coffee." She stared straight ahead.

"It is." The hot liquid's steam floated up and around my nose. I let the smell wake up my brain as I took a deep sniff. "It's very good." I took a sip and set the cup back down in front of me. I drummed my fingers on the counter. "So, you want to tell me about what went on in there?"

"I told you not to let her in. I had to get the cake made before she got here. When you let her in, I wasn't ready and I didn't want to hear her trying to tell me what to do." She motioned for me to refill her cup. "When she stomped in, she started fussing about her nephew and how he told her that he was with you and Lilith the night he was drunk." Auntie lifted the cup to her mouth and took a drink. "I knew it wasn't true. You have Mick and that nephew of hers isn't Lilith's type."

"I don't have Mick." It was apparent that with all the women Mick dated, none of them were like me. We were only partners. "We are friends. As for Brian, he deserved what Lilith did to him."

"What do you mean?" Auntie asked. "Are you telling me that you did have something to do with that boy?"

"I didn't." I knew it was best to keep my mouth shut. This was Lilith's problem. I had my own issues to deal with. "But if you don't get in there, there won't be any food for the customers."

The sounds of beating, banging of pots and running water came from the kitchen.

"Is that real bacon I smell?" My nose lifted and wrinkled trying to wrap my brain around the smell.

Since Auntie used mostly magic to create the tasty food, we created smells to smell like a real diner. Everything about The Brew was magic.

"Pish posh." Auntie spat and curled her nose. "I told her that she was in charge of the menu today and she was the one who was going to cook."

"Really cook?" I asked with fear of her answer.

"Yep." Auntie dragged her chin up and down.

Joe knocked on the diner door. He had the stack of diner rugs propped up on his shoulder and a laundry bag strapped across him.

I got up and walked over to the door.

"Good morning." I held the door for him.

"Mornin'," he said in a flat voice as his eyes focused on Auntie Meme. "What's wrong, good lookin'?"

His main focus was to get over to her and see why she was sitting out in the diner when she never ever sat out here.

"I'm taking a day off." She grabbed the remote control and flipped the TV on. "Now, put them rugs in the kitchen like you always do and make no fuss over that crazy woman in there cooking."

Joe looked at me as if I could explain Auntie's words and I shrugged. He knew I had no control over her. He focused on the swinging door as though he was scared to see what was on the other side. He dropped the laundry bag from around his body on the floor. He ventured ahead.

There were some murmurs that were followed up by laughter. Auntie Meme perked up. Her eyes narrowed before she propped herself up on her elbows to look into the kitchen window to see what was going on in her kitchen.

I tucked in my lips to keep from chuckling and walked over to the laundry bag to get out the aprons and put them away before the breakfast crowd got here, which was any minute.

"Have a good day." Joe rushed back through the swinging door with a giddy-up in his step.

"What?" Auntie Meme rolled around on the stool. "You aren't staying?"

"Nah. I've got work to get done since I've got a date with Gladys after she gets off work." Joe's face lit up in a smile.

"A what?" Auntie Meme gasped.

"I couldn't wait forever for you." He shoved the diner door open and scurried out.

Auntie Meme wasn't happy. She stared ahead. I wasn't sure if she was in shock or just plumb mad. My phone chirped a text and the noise seemed to make her snap out of the daze she was in.

She smacked her palms on the counter, firmly using them to stand.

"I've had enough." Her lips tightened. "I'm going to take back my diner and my life."

"Umm. . ." I looked at my text. "Can you take back your life without me today? I've got a meeting."

Burt had texted and asked me to come in and talk about the case.

"Something ain't right with this world. Joe has lost his marbles. You can't work at the diner. Your mom has lost her oomph for decorating. I have to call a special meeting of the Spell Circle." She shook her head and shoved through the swinging door.

"Get out! Get out of my diner and take those stupid cakes with you!" Moments later Auntie Meme's scream was followed up by Mrs. Hubbard huffing it through the diner and Auntie running after her waving a pan above her head. "Tell your nephew that he better watch it or I'll do more to him than Lilith did!"

My head dropped along with my stomach.

"You." She pointed the pan at me. "You go too!"

Chapter Thirteen

"Good morning, Patsy." I greeted the receptionist at the undercover SKUL headquarters with a coffee and one of Mrs. Hubbard's mini-cakes.

Before Auntie actually let me leave The Brew, she forced me to take any and all that remained of the cakes Mrs. Hubbard had been making or that Auntie had made before Mrs. Hubbard had shown up. She said that she didn't care if Mrs. Hubbard saw Mom do magic with her own eyes, Mom was on her own for the Belgravia Court Historic Homes Christmas Tour and it was her own fault for trying to decorate outside of her realm.

I wasn't about to fuss with Auntie so I just nodded.

"For me?" Pasty asked as she drew back.

"Come on, Patsy." I had to make peace with the woman somehow if I was going to continue to work here. "I'm on the payroll. Granted, I'm not as important as most of the agents around here, but I do work here and we might as well get along."

She stood up and opened the bag. The smell was divine. I sure was going to miss Mrs. Hubbard's cakes.

"Alright." She pulled the mini-cake out of the bag. "Is this from your family's diner?"

"It is. Well, that's no longer on the menu. But they are delicious." I took one of the to-go coffee cups out of the cardboard coffee caddy and set it on her desk.

"Mmmm." She slowly chewed and clearly enjoyed the cake. She asked with a muffle of food in her mouth, "Why did you pull these from the menu?"

"Long story, but they are being replaced with something better." I smiled with a little trepidation in my gut.

I had no idea what Auntie had planned for the day or the food. I'd never seen anyone get to her like Mrs. Hubbard. Today, Mrs. Hubbard really threw Auntie for a loop.

"Have a good day." I grabbed the coffee caddy and headed on down the hall to the secret elevator door.

"Wow, someone made a new friend." Mick turned the corner just as the elevator doors opened. "Patsy and you are going to be best friends if you keep bringing her food from the diner."

"I had to make peace with her somehow." We stepped in and I pushed the button to the basement.

"What are you doing here so early?" Mick asked.

"I'm not sure. Burt asked me to come to a meeting." I lifted the coffee container. "I did bring you a coffee and a mini-cake."

"He asked to see me too." Mick took a coffee. "Thanks, Maggie," Mick said, but the tone of his voice told me he was lost in his head probably wondering why I was being called to the meeting when Burt had only asked for my opinion on the files.

"How was your night?" I asked knowing he'd probably been up all night since Burt had officially taken his badge.

"You know. I tossed and turned." He picked a mini-cake.

"I'm sure we will get this solved in no time." I stepped out of the elevator doors and we walked down to Burt's office where I could see through the glass wall that he and Sherry were waiting for us.

"I hope so. I told Big that I'd have dinner with him tonight after he insisted because he's got something very important to tell me. We are going to The Derby first for a drink." He put his arm on mine and stopped me right before we went into the room. "Say, Maggie, why don't you go with me to meet up with Big."

"Oh, I don't know, Mick." I wasn't sure if I could handle much more of Big Stevenson.

"I really could use some backup," he said.

"Back up?" I asked before Burt opened the door to his office.

Mick pinched his lips and offered a thin smile.

"Good morning, you two." Burt looked between Mick and me. "I'm getting used to seeing both of you together."

"Good morning, sir." I ducked my head and walked straight past them, setting the coffees and bag of goodies on Burt's desk. "My auntie Meme sends her regards."

"Thank your auntie for us." Burt rubbed his hands together and picked a coffee as did Sherry. "I called you all here today because as you both know," he gestured to me and Sherry, "Mick has been given a leave of absence. I'm still allowing him to use his office and do some office work, but as far as undercover work, I've pulled all cases."

Mick stood in the back of the room. His presence was so large that I was well aware he was there.

"In any case, I've asked him to give me list of women he's dated in the past because there are no leads to the killer or ties between the victims but him. I fear these women are in danger." Burt took a mini-cake out of the bag and took a big bite.

"How are we going to help out, sir?" I asked.

"I'd like for you and Sherry to call or call on each of the women." He stopped talking when his office door opened.

"I'm sorry, Burt." A man that looked to be in his sixties with forehead creases, crow's feet and thinning hair wearing a three-piece suit said, "I'm looking for Mick."

Burt pointed to the back of the room since the man hadn't opened the door wide enough to notice Mick was in the room.

"Mick, you are late." The man tapped his watch.

"This is ridiculous, Artie," Mick gave the man a hostile glare. "I'm fine. I don't need a shrink to tell me anything that I don't already know. Besides, I thought you went into research on agents who have lost their minds."

"Mick, you agreed. That was part of why Burt has let you keep your desk job." Artie Littleman was the SKUL psychiatrist.

"I agreed to talk to a doctor. Not Artie." Mick pointed at the new arrival. "What good is he going to do me for a couple of months? He's retiring at the end of the year."

"You can go with Artie or you can go on home and not be informed at all," Burt said in a stern voice.

"Whatever." Mick stalked to the door following Artie and slammed it behind him.

"He's losing it, sir." There was a frightful look in Sherry's eyes. "In all my years of being his partner, I've never seen him this on edge."

"He has to get help and he has no choice. Now back to the plan." Burt walked around the desk.

"Help for what?" I asked.

As far as I could tell, Mick Jasper was a wonderful agent and nothing that Vinnie had given me alluded to anything different.

"What did you think of the files?" Sherry diverted from my line of questioning to her questioning me.

It was my cue that what Burt was talking about was none of my business. . .yet.

"Well, nothing really stood out to my untrained civilian eye." I made sure that I kept my witchy reality a secret. "Only the obvious. Mick Jasper. Which does make me believe that the killer is choosing the victims based on Mick and he's not making any secrets or trying to cover it up."

I had no idea where that train of thought had come from, but I did know that I hadn't used any witchy means to get it.

"Are you saying that the killer wants to be found?" Burt asked.

"Ridiculous." Sherry *tsked.*

"No it's not." Burt rubbed his chin. "The killer is only out to hurt Mick. He is willing to kill however many women that are related to Mick to not only make Mick look like the killer, but to also hurt Mick emotionally."

"That's right, sir." I nodded hoping something else would come to me. "Which is why it's important that we contact those women you asked Mick to give us the names of. Me and Sherry can divide them up and either go see them or call them."

"We don't have that kind of time. Our Mick Jasper has been a Casanova back in the day and these are just the tip of the iceberg." He held out a few pages of names of women, their address, and their phone numbers.

"Let's get through these and see what we come up with. Find out if they've been contacted by anyone. Run their phone numbers and cell numbers, cross reference them to see if there are any similar numbers calling them." Burt instructed us what to do. "Sherry, you know what to do. I'm sure Maggie is a quick learner."

"Oh, I am." I nodded my head.

"Another person we are having a hard time finding is Georgette Treminski. She's come up missing." Burt sighed.

I looked away and tried to hide the big lump in my throat.

"If she shows up dead, that will be the first person not associated with dating Mick." Burt paused. "At least that we know."

Sherry snickered.

"If she's alive, then she's running or hiding." Burt extended his arm. "Here," he handed me a couple of pages. My stomach churned when I looked at the names. Mick had been an awfully busy man. I recalled his landlord telling me a few months back that his door was revolving, but I didn't know that it never stopped revolving. "I even had Human Resources make you your own cubby out there. You can use the public computer to find out some basic information about these women. Sherry will show you to the cubicle."

"Thank you, sir." I nodded and followed Sherry out the door. It was the first time I'd had my own desk and it was exciting, only I was going to use my own way of finding out information.

Vinnie.

Everyone was so busy in the office, that no one really seemed to care what the others were doing, which made it easier for me to contact Vinnie through the necklace. The cubicle wasn't as fun and fancy as I pictured an agent's cubicle to be. It was basically a steal box with a computer, printer, pad of paper and a pen holder with pens and pencils. Stuff I didn't need anyway.

I ran my hand along my necklace and when I felt a small spark, I knew Vinnie had connected with me. With one hand, I dragged my finger down the list of names Burt had given me and with the other hand, I touched the red gem, giving Vinnie the information he needed.

"I'm looking for any commonalities besides Mick," I whispered on an exhale and looked around.

A few people were walking around so I placed my hands on the keyboard to look busy. My mind was still occupied to as why Mick was needing so much help so I decided to use the computer to see what was in there about Mick.

The search box immediately opened when my fingers touched the keyboard. I looked over both shoulders before I typed in Mick Jasper. The computer screen started to flash and an alarm sounded from the speakers.

"Code alert," the computer said as the alarm continued to beep and the screen continued to flash. "Code alert."

"Code alert?" I started to type stuff in like my name, but nothing happened just the beeping. "Code alert. . ." I stared at the screen. "Diggity Dog." I remembered Sherry telling me her code name and numbers. I quickly typed them in and the alarm stopped.

"Are you okay, Maggie?" One of the other SKUL agents popped up over my cubicle wall.

"Oh, yeah." I waved him off. "I'm fine."

Fine, nothing. If Burt or anyone else found out that I had this code, not only would my Life's Journey be taken from me, so would Sherry's.

A database screen opened up with a search box. With a hen peck, I typed in Mick Jasper so I wouldn't mess up and to make sure it was right the first time.

When Mick's file appeared on the screen, there was a date box. I decided to start from the very beginning and it was there where his career in the Army had started and his first contact with SKUL. If I read it correctly, during his last tour of duty, Mick was in charge of a special operation where it appeared someone in the platoon had gone rogue and decided to sell intelligence to the enemy. Mick was on a team of four: him, two other men—Robert Gazda and George Hill—along with a woman, Marjorie Steepleton. The report went on to say that Mick was cleared of the wrongful death of the woman, Sergeant Major Marjorie Steepleton. I dug deeper and the locked documents were classified, meaning the true findings were never released. In reality, Mick wasn't supposed to be on the front line with Marjorie during the raid. Robert Gazda and Marjorie Steepleton had the morning assignment. According to Mick's statement and the military log, Robert Gazda went AWOL, leaving Marjorie on the line alone. It wasn't until Mick realized through Marjorie's communication that she was alone and rushed to meet up with her but it was too late. Enemy fire had already taken her down. Robert Gazda had never been found. The military had even accused Mick of helping Robert, but after his log was confirmed, Mick had an airtight alibi. Mick was under a microscope for two years until the charges were dropped. It was then that Mick decided to come home and become a SKUL agent.

My heart ached for Mick. It was a hard secret about his life to keep. No wonder he had to see Dr. Artie. There was way more to uncover than Mick wanted to admit.

Quickly I wrote down the names of his secret operative group and shut the computer off when I heard Mick's voice coming down the line of cubicles. He was talking with the doctor and stopped shy of me.

They had a verbal agreement that Mick would come back in the morning and Mick promised he'd keep the appointment.

"You must think I'm a head case." Mick leaned up against my cubicle wall and folded his arms across his blue button down.

"Not at all. I think we all need professional help sometimes. And if I were in your shoes and the only thing that connected the murder of people was me, then I'm sure I'd be a basket case." I dragged the papers off the desk and handed them to him. "You've been a busy man."

"I'm not a hermit, but that was a long time ago." He looked around. "Are you busy?"

"Well," I wasn't busy but hopefully Vinnie was. "No, why?"

"Let's go grab some early lunch at The Brew. I could use an ear to talk to. Plus." He rubbed his stomach. "I've been dying for some of your auntie's beans and cornbread."

Chapter Fourteen

Auntie Meme must've called in Mom for reinforcement for the diner. When Mom saw Mick and I walk in and sit down at the corner table at the front window, she rushed over and slinked down into the empty chair next to me.

"Let me tell you, I can see why you and Lilith hated working for that woman." Mom pushed back her long black hair. She was an older version of me. Most of the time people mistook us for sisters instead of mother and daughter.

"Thank you for coming to help her. She and Mrs. Hubbard had a big blow up before I left." I leaned over. "And Joe asked Mrs. Hubbard on a date."

"No wonder she's dirtying up every towel in the diner. She has a pile this high." Mom lifted her hand in the air above the table. "She keeps telling me to remind her to call Joe and have him pick up the laundry as soon as the lunch crowd starts to die down."

"You can't do that." I warned Mom. "That's when he's meeting up with Mrs. Hubbard."

"Then I can get some decorating done." She smiled and snapped her finger.

"Mom," I whispered and looked under my eyelids at Mick as I nodded my head.

"Oh, you know." Mom looked at Mick. "I have to decorate when Mrs. Hubbard isn't home because she will be nosy and try to duplicate my artistic ability."

"I saw the entrance the other night and it was really neat." Mick was kind to my family and I appreciated that, but we had business to discuss.

"Mom, can we get two bowls of the special?" I asked.

"Cornbread and beans?" She asked with raised brows.

"Yes, please." Mick scooted his chair closer to the table. "And a Coke."

"Make that two," I said when she got up.

Even though I knew Auntie Meme and Mom could listen in on everything Mick and I were talking about, I felt better being as far away from the kitchen as possible.

"What exactly happened when you found Angela?" Mick asked.

"And I mean everything. The look on her face. The look in her eyes. Nothing is too small." Mick uncurled the silverware from the napkin and placed the napkin on his lap.

I loved his good southern manners. Within seconds, Mom was coming back out with a tray filled with the food. I glanced across the diner to the kitchen window where Auntie Meme had her head stuck out the pass through and was looking back at us. My eyes slid down to the food and then back to her. She wouldn't hesitate to put some sort of spell on Mick or me like she did the rest of the customers.

She waved a hand at me and gave me an annoyed look as if she was telling me all was fine.

"It's all good." Mom's eyes squinted when she smiled.

"It is all good." Mick leaned over the bowl and smelled.

"It better be," I warned.

"So?" Mick picked up a piece of his fried cornbread and crumbled it up into his soup beans. "Tell me word for word what happened."

"I told Burt and the police. I had the package from Mystic Couture and I went straight to her penthouse," I said.

"About that." Mick lifted a finger at me and took a quick drink. "In the video footage, the concierge is clearly seen stopping you but when I asked him about it, he said he didn't remember you."

"Really?" I shrugged. "He was a little old."

"He's in his fifties. He's not old. He's been working there since he was twenty. He knows the job inside and out. He said that there was no way you could've gotten up there without him letting you up."

"The police already have the video?" I wanted to throw him off his scent. He was digging.

"No." He shook his head. "I have sources and I wanted to see for myself."

"I went up and knocked on her door. My art." A terrifying realization washed over me. "My art!"

I threw my hand over my mouth when I realized I'd yelled it.

"Your art?" Mick leaned over the table and whispered.

"She opened the door and I reintroduced myself. I had set the package on floor because it was heavy." I pretended to go through the motions with empty hands. "She opened the door. Her face was blank. Her eyes were dark. She wasn't the smiling, bubbly person she seemed to be when I'd met her at the St. James Art Festival. She was sorta slumped. She said, '*The Ville*'."

"She actually said *The Ville*?" he asked. He stared at me, baffled. "That is important, Maggie."

He shoved his chair from the table and threw the napkin in the bowl.

"Where are you going?" I asked and wondered what I needed to do.

"I'm going to go find Georgette and find Angela's paintings." He stood up. "Well, are you coming?"

"Yeah." I waved to Mom and Auntie Meme and headed out the diner door. "I won't be home for supper."

I knew that if I didn't show up at five o'clock supper time, Mom or Auntie Meme would send the familiars after me.

"Let's take Vinnie." I suggested since he was conveniently parked in front of the diner.

"I thought you parked on the side." He pointed with a confused look on his face. "You know what," he shook his head, "I think Dr. Artie might be right."

"You mean Dr. Littleman, the psychiatrist?" I asked.

"Yeah. Everyone calls him Dr. Artie, by his first name." Mick and I got into the car. Vinnie started his engine as we went through the pretend motions. "He said that when an agent has a traumatic experience in their lives plus all the pressures of the job they can just explode. My mind isn't working right. I swear I saw you park over there."

He pointed to the side of the building when we passed it. While he was looking down the street, I tapped Vinnie's screen because the list of women we were looking up were on his circuit board and Mick didn't need to see that.

I gripped the wheel a little harder than normal because I wanted Vinnie to behave. Mick was having a hard time because of my (and Vinnie's) shenanigans, but I felt confident that if we solved this crime spree against him he'd return back to normal.

"I'm sure you are fine," I assured him. It wasn't like I could say that I knew he was fine because I'm a witch and he wasn't seeing things or imagining them.

"I still can't believe they are making me see Artie, which makes me think even more that I'm not thinking clearly." His voice held tension. "I just don't understand what I did to someone to kill these women. I must've done something awful."

"You didn't do anything." It was hard to see him struggling. "You are a good man. A kind man that wouldn't hurt anyone."

Vinnie's engine roared with displeasure.

"I'm sorry. I shouldn't say those things." I wished I could take those words back.

"No, I'm glad to have someone believe in me. Especially you." His words made my heart lurch madly. "I mean we are partners." Out of the corner of my eye I could see his smile.

"We're here." I broke the conversation. Not only because I wasn't sure what Vinnie would do but also because we needed to solve this case. Vinnie parked the car and I grabbed my purse from the behind the seat. Not that I carried a purse often, but it looked mortal. "I bet Georgette is here."

I hadn't seen Georgette since Lilith did the reversal spell. The spell had worked on her physical person, but I really had to believe that it worked on her memory and she didn't remember me at all. Even the part where we went to get coffee before the Spell Circle performed their little spell.

"Rascal," Mick greeted the concierge that I'd put to sleep. "This is Maggie Park who I was telling you about."

Rascal yawned when he saw me. He lifted his fist to cover his mouth and shook his head saying he didn't recognize me.

"Is Georgette up there?" Mick asked.

"Gosh," Rascal yawned. "I'm sorry. I have no idea why I'm so tired." He closed his eyes tight and reopened them. "She came in late last night and I haven't seen her since."

"Get some rest, buddy." Mick smacked Rascal on the arm and we headed to the elevator.

Mick didn't need Rascal's key to get us up to the penthouse. He had his own key to do that. Before I'd started to work for SKUL, I had no idea how agents and spies worked. They had access to so much.

The elevator opened up to the penthouse floor right in front of Angela's door. Mick knocked a couple of times before we heard the locks on the door unlock and Georgette stood on the other side with a big carrot stuck in her mouth and a bag of them in her hand.

"What do you two want?" She bit down and chomped. The spell had been reversed but it didn't do much on her appearance. Her hair was messy, she had on a pair of pajamas and a pair of slippers.

"We've come to talk to you," Mick said.

"I've told all the cops everything I know," she said, shoving a carrot in her mouth and shutting the door before Mick stopped it with the toe of his shoe.

"We aren't cops." He nudged me. "Flash her your badge."

"Oh, yes." I dug down in my purse and hunted around for the badge. "I'm sorry." I threw my purse toward Mick so he could hold it and I could dig deeper. "It's in here somewhere."

I lied. I kept the badge in Vinnie. Deep within my purse, I snapped my finger and pulled out the badge that'd magically appeared at the bottom of my purse.

"We are here with SKUL." He made it sound so much better than just being a cop.

"Whatever." She pulled the door open and walked back into the penthouse.

We followed her. There were squares of all different sizes that were wrapped in brown paper and tied with twine.

"Are these Angela's paintings?" Mick asked.

"Yes." Georgette chomped down on another carrot. "The gallery wants them back as soon as possible so as soon as the curator comes then I'm going to get out of here myself and head back to New York."

"You live in New York?" I asked and dragged my finger along the tops of the packaged paintings.

"Yes. Why?" she asked with a snarl on her face.

"It seems that if you were Angela's assistant that you'd live with her in Paris." I simply stated a fact.

"Angela lived in New York. All of this Paris bullshit was just that." She shook her head and flung herself down on the couch. "Trust me, there's a lot about her that you don't know."

"Oh, yeah." Mick played along. "Why don't you tell us."

"Why should I?" She curled her legs up under her knees.

"I don't know, maybe to help us not think that you killed her." I threw it out there to see if she'd take the bait.

"Like I had anything to do with killing her." She rolled her eyes. So much for taking the bait. "I have an alibi."

"Where did you go missing to yesterday?" Mick asked.

"I've been right here, wrapping up the paintings." Her stare was blank, she never blinked. "You mustn't have been looking too hard for me."

I wanted so desperately to remind her that she followed me in her car the other day and she wanted to know who killed Angela. I remembered her saying that she had information that could help.

"Do you know anything about who or why anyone would want to kill her?" I asked and sat down next to her. I pointed to the bag of carrots. "May I?"

"Sure." She shifted the bag toward me and I took one. "I know that she was in some big insurance problem."

"Like what?" I asked.

"I don't know. She was awfully private about it. I overheard her talking about if the painting is discovered, she'd be ruined. And how somebody was demanding all of this money from her."

"Franklin Bingo?" Mick asked.

"That's it. Franklin Bingo. He'd come to see her and they fought. After that was when she changed." Her eyes popped open. "He showed up here the other day."

"He did?" I asked. "Was he wearing a black hat and coat?"

"Yes. That's right." She nodded. "He wanted to see her but I told him that she was busy. She was getting ready to go to Mystic Couture for her photo shoot." Her hand flew up to her mouth. "I completely forgot to tell the police about it."

"We will take it from here." Mick motioned for me to come on. "Say, is *The Ville* in here?"

"Yes." She pointed to the big package propped up on the backside of the couch. "That's it."

"Don't let anyone move these until you hear from me." Mick instructed her. "Orders from SKUL."

She nodded.

When we were safely outside of the hotel room and in the elevator, I said, "You can't tell her she can't have them moved."

"Why not?" he asked.

"You are on leave," I reminded him.

"She doesn't know that." A wry smile crossed his lips that made my pulse suddenly leap with excitement.

Chapter Fifteen

Mick wanted to go run more checks on Franklin Bingo which was his way of telling me that he was going to go do it without me since he was the real agent and I was the civilian agent, which was fine with me because it gave me an opportunity to head over to his apartment and try to find anything from his past that would link him to the crimes.

It seemed that this Franklin Bingo could be a viable suspect but it still didn't explain what the other dead women in Mick's life had to do with Franklin.

After I dropped him off at the diner to grab his car, I went inside to check on Auntie Meme and Mom. I sent Vinnie off on his own spying mission to see where Mick had gone so when Vinnie came back to pick me up, we could hurry over to Mick's and take a look around.

"Out of the way." Auntie Meme hustled around me at the front door with a big sack of laundry hoisted over one shoulder and a takeout sack on the other arm.

"Don't try to stop her," Mom called out from behind the counter.

I stepped out of the way just in time to avoid being barreled over by her.

"She hates Gladys so much that she'd date Joe just so Gladys can't." Mom wiped down the counter and I locked the diner door behind Auntie Meme.

I watched out the window as she tried to hurry down the sidewalk toward Farmer's Dry Cleaners and wobbled right and left to keep the food steady.

"I haven't seen her move that fast without a little magical help in a long time." I laughed and watched until she was out of my vision. I turned around. "Spell in the food?"

"I guess. She was back in there all day perfecting whatever it is that Joe Farmer claimed to love. But you know as much as I do that if true love isn't meant to be then it's not meant to be." She threw the towel in the sink behind the counter and leaned on the counter propping herself up on her elbows. "Speaking of love."

"You can get any ideas out of your head." I pulled a clean coffee mug out of the rack of dishes and poured a cup of coffee. "I mean, he is adorable."

"Adorable? He's a hunk." Mom sighed. "And since I know now that he's part of your Life's Journey, then it might be a good thing."

Just another example of my mom being able to completely shock me.

"He's a mortal." I reminded her how dangerous it could be.

"He's a smart mortal that just might be the one you can confide in." Mom flipped around and leaned back on the counter with her arms folded. "After all, there will be a lot of SKUL investigations where they are going to need you and him."

"Not if I can't figure out what's going on." I stared out over the diner.

"Can I help?" Mom asked. I looked at her. "If not, I'm a good listener."

"Three women who have been involved with Mick as more than just friends have been murdered. He is the only link between the victims. One of them was that Angela Fritz from the art festival." It did feel good talking to someone other than Mick about it. I felt like I couldn't be open with him since it did involve such an intimate past with the women.

"The same lady that didn't show up for Lilith?" Mom asked.

"Yes. She didn't show up because someone was stabbing her with a knife in her back. Long story short, I found her and I also found out that she's tied to Mick like the rest of the women, only he's left that little part out. So while he's off trying to find out who killed her, I'm working for SKUL because they gave him a leave of absence."

"Something tells me that his past has crept up to haunt him." Her words were truer than she could imagine.

"Unfortunately, I think you are right." I put away my coffee cup when Vinnie pulled up at the sidewalk. "Vinnie followed Mick after I dropped him off here to make sure he wasn't going home like he said so I can go by his apartment and look around, see if I can find anything that ties to his past."

"Good thinking." Mom showed the first bit of pride on her face since she'd learned I worked for SKUL. "This is your Life's Journey. You will figure this out."

"I know. I just hate that he has to go through this." I walked around the counter and gave Mom a hug and a kiss on her cheek.

It was the first time we'd had a real grown-up talk since I took my Life's Journey. It was the first time I felt like she'd taken me seriously. It felt good.

"That was a touching scene," Vinnie said when I'd gotten in the car.

"It's a funny thing how relationships work, Vinnie." I strapped on seat belt. He veered out into the downtown traffic. "Especially between the parent and child and when the parent recognizes the child is no longer a child but an adult."

"That seems all too complicated for me, Maggie. But I did get the list completed and happy to say that each woman on there is still alive. Some of them do not live here. It seems to me that we need to be focusing on the person with the black hat," Vinnie said.

"I haven't seen them around since the hotel when Angela was murdered, so I have to wonder if her murder is unrelated." It was a scenario I had wanted to go over with Mick but he seemed too preoccupied and stressed. It was one last thing he needed to fill in his head. "I can't help but think that the black hat person has something to do with Mick and the other women, but Angela Fritz is the only one that had something to do with *The Ville* painting since Franklin Bingo has claimed she stole it from him. It just so happens that she too was involved with Mick, only no one knows about him and Angela."

"No one that we know of, Maggie." Vinnie passed Farmer's Dry Cleaners.

I looked into the window and Auntie Meme had her arms lifted in the air as if she was about to bring a spell down.

"Stop!" I yelled and jumped out into downtown traffic as soon as Vinnie came to a stop. "Pull over," I instructed him through the beeping of horns and people rolling down their windows to yell at the crazy lady, me.

Auntie had poor Joe pinned up against the wall inside the cleaners where luckily there weren't any customers.

"Auntie," I scolded her when I walked in. "What are you doing?"

"Oh honey," she greeted me with a sweet smile and brought her hands down to her side. "Just a little spell to turn this prince back into a pumpkin that we can put in the pumpkin pies at The Brew." She swung her arms up again.

"Joe?" I waved my hand in front of his face. He didn't move, blink, or speak. He was comatose. "Are you nuts? What am I saying?" I ran my hand over my face. "Of course you are nuts."

"I am not." She protested. "I'm tired of Gladys Hubbard. And it's either turn Joe into something and let her live or vice versa."

"Or neither. And I opt for neither." I dragged her arms down to her side. "Joe has been trying to woo you for years. It's your fault that he's now turned to Mrs. Hubbard."

"No, it's your fault for telling us about those cakes and having her at the diner where Joe has met her." Auntie did have all the facts straight. "But, I'm willing to forgive if you make everything go back to the way it was a week ago. Me at the diner making all the food. Joe coming in and cat-calling me while I ignore him and you off doing your little spy game."

"You let Joe out of his coma and I'll be sure to check on them during their date. I can do a little spell to insure that this is their only date." I pointed to Joe. "Now, undo him."

Auntie huffed, snorted and pouted her way through letting Joe off the hook and when he came to, it was as if nothing happened.

"This is a change." Joe noted when he saw all the laundry that needed to be dry cleaned. "I would've come down to get it."

Auntie looked at me and I urged her to be nice.

"Fine," she spat. "I had a lot since Gladys Hubbard didn't know what she was doing and made a complete mess of my kitchen before I kicked her out. I need these by tomorrow."

I wasn't pleased with Auntie's way of giving Mrs. Hubbard a kick in the gut, but at least I got some sense knocked into her.

"I guess I'll get a firsthand taste of her cookin'." Joe hoisted the laundry bag up on his shoulder before he flung it into a big cart. "But I sure bet she's not better than you, Meme. After all, you are the one with the diner."

"You got that right." That seemed to pep her up. "Let's get back to work." She grabbed me by the arm. "Will I see you in the morning, Joe?" she asked. "Biscuits and gravy."

"You betcha." Joe winked, giving Auntie Meme a little giddy-up in her step.

I never thought I was going to get Auntie Meme out of Vinnie. She fussed and cursed letting all sorts of sparks and flames shoot from the tips of her fingernails and hair on the way back to The Brew. There was no way I was going to let her walk back in fear she'd change her sudden slightly better disposition about Joe and Mrs. Hubbard's date.

"You promise?" she asked before I could shove her out of Vinnie.

"I promise after I go do what I need to for SKUL," which was go to Mick's apartment, "then I will make sure to stop by Mrs. Hubbard's and check on their late lunch date. But you have to get out of the car or I will miss their date completely."

"Do you remember your family crest?" She threw up the family, coven, and thyself. "Family always comes first."

"Do you remember no magic in public due to witch hunts? Get out." On that cue Vinnie opened the door.

"Miss Kitty has never been this mean to you." She jabbed her finger in Vinnie's dash before she got out.

Mom stood at the door shaking her head, knowing that if I had to bring Auntie back that something horrible had happened and I'd leave it up to Auntie to tell her. Not that Auntie Meme thought what she did was wrong, she didn't.

Chapter Sixteen

"Where did Mick go?" I asked Vinnie as soon as he pulled out from The Brew.

I wasn't about to stick around to give Mom the low down or even see if Auntie Meme would come clean about what she'd done to poor old Joe Farmer.

"Well, Maggie, he went back to SKUL headquarters where I used my radar to follow him up to his office." Vinnie's circuit screen rolled footage of Mick going into his office, which dawned on me that I'd never been in his office.

I'd only been in Burt's office and the guts of the basement where they'd put me in the cubicle, which reminded me of Sergeant Major Marjorie Steepleton.

"Vinnie," I watched as Mick sat at his desk going through some files, "I need you to look up Sergeant Major Marjorie Steepleton. Mick didn't tell me, but she and he were in Special Forces together and she was killed."

"Why is this of any importance?" Vinnie asked.

"I don't know, I'm just trying to not only uncover his past to see if there is a link between him and her intimately, if she's one of the reasons he throws himself into his work and part of the demons Dr. Artie seems to think he's battling." I really needed to get back to SKUL and get on the computer to figure out exactly what was in Mick's file.

There had to be something there. There was an inkling in my twitching nose that I couldn't exactly scratch.

"I'll do a little digging around while you be careful digging around in there." Vinnie pulled up to Mick's apartment building.

Mrs. Cartmell, Mick's landlady, was sitting on the front porch on an old metal chair. She had on the same blue housedress I'd seen her in last time with the same thick-soled white nurse's shoes and knee-high pantyhose.

"I don't know what it is about you women and that man." She rose a bushy brow when I approached.

"Hi, Mrs. Cartmell. It's great to see you again." I nodded and tried to be as polite as I could and get past her. "We are just work friends. Nothing more," I assured her.

She had other plans.

"Seriously, he must be one fine used car salesman." She *tsked* and crossed her arms across her chest, looking over the small lawn out front.

"Excuse me? Used car salesman?" I asked.

"Mick's job. At least for this week." She pursed her lips. "I've never seen a man have so many jobs. One week he sells fish at the pet shop. The next week he's a chef and now he's a used car salesman. Which you should know since you work together."

"Yes." I nodded realizing that Mick really didn't tell all those women that he was an undercover agent for SKUL and that the murders had to be tied to his SKUL job. But how? "I have to run up and get a car title he left here. Good to see you."

I didn't leave any room for her to continue to make conversation. Something in his past had crossed with his SKUL job—that was the one thing about this case I was sure of.

When I got up to Mick's apartment, the first thing I did was call Sherry from Mick's phone.

"Hello?" She sounded strange.

"Sherry, it's Maggie Park." I glanced around the very clean apartment and wondered exactly where Mick might keep anything personal. I was here so I might as well look into his background and completely rule it out.

"Oh, Maggie," relief over took her voice. "I saw it was Mick's number and I had just seen him leaving his office. I knew he couldn't have made it home that fast."

"Where was he going?" I asked.

"I'm not sure. He was pretty upset because the police really do want to charge him with the murders of those women." She paused. "I'm afraid we are running out of time."

"I have a hunch," I said.

"A hunch?" Sherry wasn't too keen on my hunches.

"They haven't been wrong so far. Just hear me out." She could either listen or hang up, either way, I was ready to give my theory. "All the women from Mick's past that are being killed off—none of those women really knew that Mick is an undercover agent for SKUL. They all think he does something else for a living. That makes me think the killer knows that he's an agent."

I tucked the phone between my shoulder and ear and walked over to the desk that was so pristine it didn't look like Mick used it. When I opened the drawer there was nothing in it. I headed back to his bedroom.

"Maggie, that's a far-fetched thought. The killer has something against Mick and it wouldn't take a special agent to figure out that Mick dates a lot of women, or to follow him to see the women." Sherry rambled on and on as I continued to look for the something that I had no idea I was looking for.

In fact, I quit listening to her, because I knew there had to be someone in the agency that was mad at Mick. It just made complete sense to me. The closet was the most logical place to look for anything Mick had packed away. At least that was where Abram Callahan stored most of his junk. There was an old blue locker trunk. I pulled it out of the closet and opened it.

"These women that were being murdered were women way back in his past, which was why we are looking at people in his past." She stopped. "You know; he did say that he was meeting with his old high school buddy. That Big guy."

Right on top was a photo of Mick and Angela at a Louisville High School football game. In the background, clearly someone who was not supposed to be the focus of the photos and who had a glare on his face, was a younger Big Stevenson and another boy.

"Oh no." I groaned when I realized that I'd told Mick I could meet him to see Big.

Big Stevenson. My mind whispered his name again, Big Stevenson.

Big Stevenson would have a jealous motive to hurt not only Angela Fritz since they used to date and she wasn't going to give him the time of day when she was here. And if he found out that she and Mick had a fling, he did seem the type to get really angry.

"I'll let you know what I find out." I hung up on her and began to search for anything else that might give me a clue into Mick's past before I had to rush out of there to meet him and Big.

There were a couple of yearbooks from high school and I grabbed the one that he'd written senior year on and put it on the floor next to me as I continued to look for anything else.

My hand raked over a stack of unbound photos where the people were dressed in their army gear. One with a girl in her camo uniform, gun, and her hair pulled back in a ponytail with a big bright smile on her face caught my attention. Mick had his arm around her and they were clearly in the desert. I flipped the photo over and read the back.

"*Always my hero. Love Marjorie.*" I flipped the photo back over and got my first look at the woman Mick seems to be haunted about. For some reason, I took that photo and put it on top of the other photo I'd taken of Angela and Mick with Big in the background and the school album.

I went back to shuffling the photos when I happened to come up on one that was of Mick, Marjorie, Angela and Big. The only one not in a blue Army uniform was Angela. She had on a blue formal gown with sequins lining the edges. I flipped it over. *Army Formal Ball* was scribbled across the back along with the names. Only Big's name wasn't Big, it was Robert Gazda.

"Big was in the Army?" I asked myself and remembered what I'd learned in the office about Robert Gazda being in the special operative group Mick was in and brought up on charges and then dismissed.

My heart started to race. Was Big the killer? All of this seemed unusual.

I moved my hand around some more to see if I could quickly find anything else. Why hadn't Mick said anything about Big being a major part of his past? What was Mick trying to cover up?

Did Big know that Mick had asked me to join them tonight? Then it occurred to me when Mick and I had seen each other at headquarters that Mick said that Big insisted he come to meet him. That he had something very important to tell him.

My imagination took over. All I could see was Big grabbing Mick by the throat and dangling him in the air as he strangled the life out of Mick.

Then suddenly I remembered the words Mick said before we'd been interrupted by Burt.

"I could use the backup."

I slammed the locker shut and pushed it back into the closet. I grabbed the photos and album and the phone. I put the phone back on the charger on my way out the door and didn't bother taking the stairs or the elevator. I put my finger next to my nose and blinked, praying I wasn't too late.

"Find what you needed?" Mrs. Cartmell asked as I darted past her.

"More than I needed!" I yelled and dove into Vinnie as he opened the door for me and he took off before I could shut it.

I glanced back at Mrs. Cartmell. She had stood up and put her hands on her hips. The confusion was written on her face about what she'd just seen. I pointed at her and looked down my finger for good aim. Slowly I circled my finger at her body as it got smaller and smaller and snapped, sending her a spell that made her even forget she talked to me.

Chapter Seventeen

"Take me to The Derby as fast as you can," I instructed Vinnie from the driver's seat. There was no time to waste. Mick was in danger and I was sure of it.

I thumbed through the album and saw plenty of pictures of Mick, Angela and Big. All chummy and friendly like.

"I found out that Marjorie and Mick did have more than a working relationship." Vinnie was supposed to give me information that I didn't know. "She was killed in the line of duty when Mick was in charge. It was his first assignment as the leader of the group, unfortunately, Marjorie was killed in the line of fire where another member was supposed to be before Mick could get to her to back her up."

"Yeah, I knew that but I wasn't sure how involved Mick was with her until I found these photos." I gripped both of them. One in each hand. Mick looked happy. A real genuine smile on his face that I wished I'd seen on him. His blue eyes were brighter and his face had a sunny outlook. "Pull up the stats on Big Stevenson and his time in the Army."

"Officer Big Stevenson was in charge of planning and directing military operations, overseeing combat activities, and served as combat leader. He was in charge of tanks and other armored assault vehicles, artillery systems, special operations, or infantry units," Vinnie said.

"He was in charge of the assault vehicles and special operations?" I asked more for me than for Vinnie to repeat it.

"There is more, Maggie," Vinnie continued. "Officer Stevenson was discharged without honor after the incident with Marjorie. What are you thinking, Maggie?" Vinnie asked and turned off the interstate toward Old Louisville.

"I'm thinking that Big has been jealous of Mick long before they joined the Army because of Angela Fritz. When he was discharged, his jealousy turned to rage because Mick was not discharged. This makes me think that Dr. Artie is right." I bit my lip and looked out the window at The Derby when we pulled up. "I can't help but think that Big is the one who just exploded without warning."

"Be careful, Maggie." I heard Vinnie say as I got out of the car after I had grabbed the photo of the happy couples at the Army ball. I stuck it in my back pocket on my way into the bar.

I glanced around at the tables and chairs inside The Derby. It was busy for a weeknight. The dark wood with mahogany wainscoting went halfway up the wall and gave the bar the artistic feel Old Louisville was known for. The rest of the walls were painted a muted green giving a warm feeling. The stage in the back of the bar already had a bunch of people standing in front of it as if they were waiting for a band to take the stage. Not one of them didn't have tattoos all over their arms and faces—really all visible skin covered.

Buck stood behind the bar and looking down the shelves that were lined with bottles and bottles of liquor, including delicious Kentucky bourbons.

"What's going on?" I asked Buck and curled up on my toes. It was going to be hard to find Mick and Big in this crowd. My necklace warmed against my chest. I put my hand up to it to acknowledge I'd gotten the message and that Big, Robert or whoever he was tonight wasn't going to take me down.

"The Grind," Buck said and poured a pale ale from the spout. "They decided to do a sound check and someone put it out there on social media." He nodded and pushed the beer toward me. "Try it. New brew."

"Great for business. And thanks." I grabbed the glass and held it up in the air to honor him. He waited for my reaction as I took a drink. "Delicious."

"Brewed right here in Louisville." He nodded. "Not bad."

I glanced over the tops of the heads of the crowd again for another look.

"Your buddy is over there playing darts." He lifted his chin in the direction of the dart boards that were near the stage in the front corner of the bar. "He's with that rodeo guy from the Cowboy Channel. Girls are going ga-ga over him."

"Thanks." I lifted the glass one more time before I took the plunge and melted into the crowd just as The Grind ripped their first cord on the electric guitar.

Arms flew up with their rock and roll fingers thrashing in the air, their heads followed. I dipped and ducked my way over to the dart boards where Mick and Big were whopping it up. My disdain for Big, Robert whoever the big lug pretended to be, was running amok.

"Hey, there." Mick smiled and took a step toward me.

"Who do you think you are?" I grabbed Big's arm before I even recognized Mick. "Big Stevenson. Robert Gazda. Whoever you think you are." I dragged the photo out of my pocket and stalked to the dark board, jabbing a dart right through his heart and making the picture stick.

"What is wrong with you, Maggie?" Mick's big blue eyes grew the size of half-dollars.

"Do you think we don't know what you did?" I motioned between me and Mick, speaking directly at Big.

"You have been jealous of Mick Jasper since high school and you think that you can just pretend like you showed up here to see Angela Fritz when you are really here to avenge your hatred—not only letting Mick take the blame for Marjorie Steepleton's death when you were the one who was supposed to be in front of her when she got killed in the line of duty. Not Mick. And you are AWOL. You killed the women and now Angela Fritz. Arrest him Mick."

"What the hell?" Big eased up to me. "Mick you better keep your piece on a leash," he warned with a snarled lip.

"Whoa," Mick stepped up and in between Big and me.

"What are you going to do, Robert? Kill me now?" I laughed.

"Maggie, stop this." Mick's voice was stern and bold. "You don't know what you are talking about."

"Oh, I know. I know that he is a killer." I jabbed my finger over Mick's shoulder. "I know that you and Angela had a little fling before you left for the Army and I know that Big here is jealous of you. People kill over jealousy and scorned love."

"That's it." Robert stepped up and took his hand to push Mick out of the way.

"Is it?" I asked and whipped my head side-to-side before I stuck a flat palm toward him, stopping him dead in his tracks.

His legs walked in place, stomping on the floor of the bar with each step. He looked down. His hands fisted and he tried harder to move forward. He glared at me with a contorted angry face.

I kept a steady hand square in front of me not letting him get another inch toward me.

"Maggie?" Mick looked between my hand and Big.

"This is messed up." Big stopped fighting his own legs and I dropped my hand. "She's a freak." He grabbed a jacket off the chair before he downed what was left of his beer.

Mick shook his head and put a finger up to me as he grabbed his phone and quickly dialed someone.

"Yeah. He's gone. He's angry." Mick curled his lips in a huff. He stared at me like I was the freak Big claimed I was. "I don't know what all that was about, but you've ruined it now."

"Ruined what?" I asked.

"Big isn't the killer, but you're right, he is AWOL and this was a plan for them to pick him up tonight." Anger plagued his face. "Now the plan is blown up."

I ran my hand over my necklace and thought about Big.

"No I haven't." I grabbed Mick by the hand and dragged him through, under and around the jumping crowd as The Grind jammed on stage.

Vinnie was waiting outside with his doors already open.

"Good evening, Maggie. Agent Jasper." Vinnie slammed the door and squealed. "I've got him on the run down the street toward Central Park. He's on foot and he's pretty burly so he shouldn't get far. Agent Jasper, you can call your people and have them meet you near the amphitheater in the park because that's where Maggie will have him waiting for them."

"I don't know what is going on, but let me out." Mick jerked the handle of Vinnie's passenger door.

"It's okay, Mick." I tried to assure him, but I could see he was trying to keep his hands from shaking and desperately trying to get out of the car. "Don't fight it. I'll explain it all."

He shoved his legs straight and dug his feet deep into the floor board as though he was trying to get away.

"Maggie, I'm not sure why you did what you did in there, but I'm feeling this wasn't a good way to let Agent Jasper know that you are a witch." Vinnie just let it all out there.

I wasn't sure what to do. It was the first time I'd actually done magic in front of a mortal that was going to remember it.

"Whhi. . . .whhiii?" Mick gulped. "This is a joke. This is some sort of joke."

"Agent Jasper, I assure you this isn't a joke. Maggie, are you okay?" Vinnie asked bringing me to the present.

"Yes. Vinnie, I need you to make sure that Robert Gazda is nicely wrapped up as if Mick had done it and please call Burt to let him know where he will be in Mick's voice of course." I gripped the wheel. I stared ahead. "Mick, I know this all seems strange to you right now, but I promise if you stay calm and not blow up when Vinnie lets you out of the car, I'll explain it all."

"You are a witch?" Mick backed away as far as he could with his back up against the door and he was facing me. "Witches are real?"

"Oh, Vinnie. I need you to erase Robert's mind of me stopping him with my palm back at the bar. He needs to have all memory of me erased, even going to the bar." I had to cover my tracks with Robert.

"Are you going to erase my mind?" Mick asked.

"I can't. I've tried." I shrugged.

"You've tried?" His voice vibrated with anxiety.

"Yep." I looked over at him. "You're safe from any spells."

"Spells?" Mick looked green around the gills. "I think I'm going to be sick. You stay away from me," he warned through gritted teeth.

"Please do not get sick inside of me, Agent Jasper." Vinnie skidded to a stop and popped Mick's door open, dumping him right on the curb next to a handcuffed Robert.

"Mick," I called from inside the car out the open door. "I'm telling you, if you try to tell anyone about what you've just seen, no one will remember but you. Then they will really force Dr. Artie to admit you to some mental institution."

"Wait." Mick got up and leaned inside the car. As he asked his questions, he looked around Vinnie as if things were coming into focus. "How did you know about Big being in the army? He changed his image. He shaved his head and got all of those tattoos. He even bulked up and decided to come a cowboy and change his name so the government couldn't find him. And Marjorie? How did you know about her? All of those documents are classified and sealed."

"I sorta got Sherry's clearance and looked it up on the SKUL computers." It was time to come clean with all of it. The flash of blue lights appeared in my rear-view. "I'm begging you. Please don't tell a word of this to anyone."

"I can't believe you. This is not real." Mick shook his head. "You stay right here and don't you move," he warned me as if I were the perpetrator. The look in his eye scared me. It was as if I was the enemy.

"I'm sorry, Mick." I tried to swallow the lump in my throat. "I can't do that."

Vinnie took off leaving Mick and Robert next to the curb. The echoes of sirens got closer and closer.

"Let's go home," I said to Vinnie as a tear trickled down my cheek.

Chapter Eighteen

All night long I tossed and turned getting zero sleep. The idea that Mick Jasper knew about who I really was made me sick to my stomach. I knew it was going to affect our relationship, but I also knew that he couldn't tell anyone. Especially Burt.

My Life's Journey helping out SKUL wouldn't be affected by the fact that Mick knew my secret. It was my Life's Journey and no mortal could keep me from it. Not even hunky Mick Jasper.

Getting out of bed and heading to The Brew to work before I made an appearance at SKUL was going to be difficult to get through. Even using magic to get me dressed wasn't fun and my jeans and black sweater matched my somber mood.

"I'm assuming you had a heck of a night." Auntie Meme greeted me when I walked into the kitchen.

"I look that good?" I asked with a thinly veiled smile.

"Let's just say that your mood is reflected in how you walked in. I'm used to my perky niece." She dragged a finger along my chin. "Mick Jasper?"

"How did you know?" I asked.

She snapped her finger turning the pots of boiling water into the specials for the day and curled her finger to follow her into the diner.

"You sit and I'll serve our coffee this morning," she instructed me and I did exactly what she said. Coffee was exactly what I needed.

"You forget that I'm your guardian of your Life's Journey so I kinda get all the notes on what's going on with that." She pushed the steaming cup of coffee in front of me and the bowl of creamers.

"I knew he'd have to know eventually." I uncurled the foil off the tops of the creamers and put two in my coffee. "I just thought I'd be telling him on my terms, not in a have-to situation."

"Sometimes things are better unplanned." She pointed to the door.

I rotated the stool I was sitting on and looked. Mick Jasper was standing at the door, looking in.

"Now is the time to explain to him. He will understand." Auntie Meme eased herself through the swinging door and disappeared into the kitchen.

With some trepidation, I got up and walked to the door. My mind reeled with what I was going to say but nothing seemed to stick in the whirlwind of thoughts. All escaping me when I unlocked the door.

All I could say was hi.

"I've been up all night and I sure could use a cup of your auntie Meme's coffee." His stare was bold and he assessed me frankly.

"We've got plenty." I figured I was just going to have to let him take the lead on where the conversation took us. I already knew the truth and it was going to be up to him to let me know what he wanted to know.

"First question, book club?" he asked. Something in his manner smoothed my frayed nerves.

"Ah, the book club." I tried not to smile as I remembered all the tricks they'd played on him. "They are actually a group of elders from different covens that make up a Spell Circle."

"Spell Circle?" His chin tucked to his chest and glared at me under his brows.

"Yes. They meet once a week to make sure all is right with the covens." I only said what I needed to say.

"The AC Cobra?" He pointed to Vinnie who was parked in his normal spot at the curb.

"My familiar." My words greeted him. His chest visibly puffed out when he sucked in a deep calming breath.

"Why don't you have a cat like *Sabrina the Teenage Witch*?" he asked with a straight face.

"Mortals have their own idea about familiars. But a familiar can be anything that fits the witch's personality. Mine so happens to be Vinnie." I looked out the door at Vinnie. His lights blinked. "My necklace," I ran my fingers across the red stone dangling around my neck, "is a direct link to him and my mom or Auntie Meme if need be. Like Rails and Nails."

I told him about the last job we'd done and how my mom was the one who could talk to animals because it was her Life's Journey to be one with nature, including all of Mother Nature's creatures.

"Life's Journey?" he asked and gave me the space to fill him in.

"All witches have what is called a Life's Journey. It's not something that a witch picks." I refilled his coffee because I knew for what I was about to tell him, he was going to need stay focused. "The day you first came to the diner, I knew there was something about you that was meant to be in my life. That night, Lilith and I were playing a little game we love called Truth or Spell. The loser tells the other what spell they need to put on someone and who that someone is. She picked you that night."

He straightened himself up and stared at me.

"When the cat spell didn't work on you and bounced to your informant, I knew something was wrong. I even tried to erase your memory, but that didn't work either." I bit the edge of my lip to stop from talking. I wanted to give him space to process what I'd told him or even to ask a question.

"Why didn't the spells work on me?" he asked.

"Because, you idiot!" Auntie Meme pushed through the door with some biscuits and gravy. She threw the plates down in front of us. "I don't have time for catching up, we have a diner to open. Now, SKUL is Maggie's Life's Journey. You are part of her Life's Journey. Any mortal part of a witch's Life Journey is immune to the spells."

She waddled over to the front door and unlocked it. Joe Farmer was already waiting.

"Now, if you have any more questions, they can wait until her shift is over." Auntie Meme looked at Joe. "Git on in here. I've got your breakfast waiting." She walked past me on the way to the kitchen and whispered, "You forgot to check on that last night."

"I'm so sorry." I pointed to Mick for my excuse and let out a deep exhale.

"Huh?" Mick looked at me.

"I was supposed to interrupt a date for her." I turned my lips into a smile when Joe sat down next to Mick.

"You are in my seat," Joe spat out the words contemptuously.

"My bad." Mick held up his hands and slid his coffee down a couple of spots and moved while I turned on the TV for the customers who were filing in.

"So, Joe," I grabbed the pot of coffee and filled up his cup. "How was your date with Mrs. Hubbard?"

"Aw, it wasn't so great." He pressed his lips together. "The food that she raved about was a little on the burnt side and gave me instant indigestion." He banged his fist on his chest. "I can't put up with that all my life. I mean, she's a nice woman and all but that little yippy mutt of hers got on my nerves too."

Auntie Meme stuck her head through the window. There was a big smile on her face.

"I'm sorry to hear that." I excused myself and walked around filling up the customers' cups before I took a few orders.

Words of mumbles and grumbles blanketed the diner as they complained about going to work or not enough sleep. Mick said he didn't have any place to go so he'd hang out there and try to get answers about my Life's Journey.

Between customers I told him about all the familiars and how Lilith's Life Journey was with the first case Mick and I worked on as partners at Mystic Couture.

A couple people who sat at the counter complained about how they had the worst weekend and today wasn't going to be any better.

"I'm sure this good home cooking of my auntie Meme's will put you right in the mood." I set their food in front of them.

With one bite, you could hear their voices take a more upbeat tone. They could see a happier outcome to the day.

Mick pointed to them and to the food and then to Auntie Meme who'd stuck her head through the kitchen window with a big grin on her face. "Her Life's Journey?"

"Yeah." I leaned on the counter. "This is why everyone feels so good after they leave. Auntie Meme feels like there is so much sadness already in the world and with the shootings around here, she figured she'd donate a little bit of happiness."

"No wonder it's always packed." He leaned down the counter where he was sitting earlier and looked at Joe. "What's his story? He's always here."

"Joe." I shook my head. "There is not a single ounce of happiness added to his food. He has straight biscuits and gravy like me and you. He's been in love with Auntie Meme for as long as I can remember." I glanced back at the kitchen window to make sure Auntie wasn't being all nosy. "There has been a turn of events," I whispered, "Joe met Mrs. Hubbard and asked her out. It didn't set well with Auntie and she was prepared to make both of them pay. That's why I was supposed to go check on them last night, but then you and I happened."

I grabbed the pot of coffee and while I let Mick digest everything I was telling him, I walked around and refilled cups and took some orders.

It took a couple of hours before the breakfast crowd had cleared and we were well on our way into the lunch hours. I had to quickly refill all the condiments on the tables and clean up any breakfast dishes before Auntie started the daily specials, which happened to be on the okra side of the vegetables. She made some seriously good fried okra and my mouth was already watering.

"Are you going to hang around here all day?" I asked Mick.

"You're the witch, you tell me." The idea of my existence seemed to be settling in his soul. There was still a nervous fidgeting as his knees bounced up and down, but all-in-all I think the news might've been sinking in and he was beginning to be more accepting.

I wagged my finger at him. "It doesn't work that way. That's the problem with you mortals." I took the soapy rag from behind the counter and did a quick swipe of the bar area before I put the paper placemats and pre-made rolled-up napkins with silverware on top of it along with the small frosty water glasses.

"So you can't just, I don't know, wiggle that finger and bring the killer to justice?" he asked. "I'd really like to put this all behind me and get to work. So go ahead." He lifted a hand. "Wiggle your little finger and make all of this go away."

"Ah." I lifted my chin. "This is the bitter and angry part where you've accepted me for me and now you want me to prove it."

"No. I want you to make it go away." He eyed me suspiciously.

"I'm sorry. I can't." I shrugged and went back to filling up the water glasses so they'd be ready as soon as a customer sat down.

"Really?" Sarcasm dripped from his mouth. "I said it early and I stand by it again. What good is all this gibberish if you can't use it."

"You wouldn't understand." I decided it was best to leave him alone.

"Try me, Maggie. I'm pretty smart," he said.

"Okay, listen and listen to me good." I put down the water pitcher and planted both hands on the counter in front of him. I leaned over really close to his face, so close his cologne made me dizzy with tingles. But I knew I had to put on my game face. "I can only do spells at certain times. It's not like we can go all willy-nilly on people. It doesn't work that way. I have a Life's Journey to help SKUL keep order in our world and somehow you are the one who is supposed to help me with that. Burt noticed that I'm pretty good at blending in and you are the one that's pretty good at solving these things. I might be able to help out in tight situations or get you to a hospital when you are hurt." I reminded him in the first few days that I'd met him how he'd been injured and Vinnie zoomed him to the hospital. "But I can't just snap a finger and make all of this disappear. Trust me, if I could, then I would make all the world hunger and other world problems go away and we'd always be living in paradise. But we live by the fate of the world. And when fate and spell collide. . ."

"It's magic," the word left his lips and kissed my soul.

Chapter Nineteen

"So let's go over this one more time." Burt sat in front of me at his desk. Sherry was in the chair next to me and Dr. Artie was in the back of the room taking notes.

Burt said that he thought it would be good for Dr. Artie to be there since he was treating Mick.

He'd called during the lunch shift to ask me to come in to discuss the whole Big situation because Mick had opened his mouth and told them I was there. I should've covered my bases and told Mick that'd I'd erased Big's memory and that he didn't recall any of it. Since Mick was put on desk duty, he'd gone up to his office to do paperwork while I met with Burt.

"It's simple. I was following up leads on the Marjorie thingy from Mick's past. I figured it'd be a good thing to check out Mick's apartment. When I went in, with Mick's permission of course." I might as well tell the truth (well partial truth anyway) on how I found the photos. "Then I put two and two together thinking that Big or Robert or whoever he is, was the killer of the other women as well as Angela Fritz because of the jealously he had of Mick."

I gulped and so wished I could tell Mick to lie for me. He was still so mad that I'd gone into his apartment without telling him. Not that he had anything to hide, but it wasn't like we were partners in life, only work.

"Did Mick tell you about Marjorie Steepleton?" Burt asked.

I shook my head.

"Then how did you know about her? That case is sealed and classified and only the agents with clearance can get that information," Dr. Artie said from behind me. "And of course me since I'm his doctor."

I looked at Burt. I didn't like Artie's tone and I didn't take orders from him. Sherry nervously shifted in her seat. Burt looked between us before his eyes settled on Sherry. She dipped her head letting her blond hair fall in her face.

Apparently, Burt wanted to hear my answer. "Go on and answer Dr. Artie's question."

I sat up in my chair and scooted to the edge before I cleared my throat and said, "Sir, I needed to find out about the women in Mick's past if I was going to do a decent job and Sherry only gave me her information to do that." I looked at her. "It's not her fault that I snooped around."

"Fine. I guess the only thing good that came out of this is the fact you noticed Big was actually Robert. I'm glad you didn't get caught in the scuffle between him and Mick." Burt seemed to believe that it was all Mick that brought Big down and that was fine by me.

"Oh yes, sir." I nodded. "I was only at the bar listening to The Grind, my favorite band when I noticed what was going on and it was him. I'm just glad I didn't screw up the undercover thing."

"How do you think Mick is going to feel about him having to turn in his longtime friend?" Burt asked Artie.

"Well, I think it's another step on closing the case in his past." Artie walked up. "But ultimately it was Mick's job to have made sure Marjorie Steepleton was safe and had back up." He looked at his watch. "Speaking of which, it's time for me to meet with Mick."

After he excused himself, Burt turned back to Sherry and me.

"Big is not the killer of the three women. He has alibis for all of them and we are back to square one." Burt closed the file on his desk. "Do you have any more suggestions?"

Sherry and I both looked at each other.

"We are still looking into the other women Mick has dated, but there are a lot so we are going to need time to go through them." Sherry was good at phrasing things to buy us time and that was exactly what I needed. Time to think and time to get Mick freed from desk duty.

After Burt excused us and I had been put in my place that I was only to call the women Mick had a past with to make sure there wasn't any unusual activity in their lives, I went up to Mick's office. It was locked up tight and I didn't see his old Caprice in the parking lot making me wonder how his appointment with Dr. Artie had gone. He was reluctant to go because he was so private about his life. Now I could see why.

I was going to be late for five o'clock supper if I didn't get out of there and I'd already been reprimanded not only by Burt but also Dr. Artie.

"Good afternoon, Maggie." Vinnie was all too cheerful. "How was your meeting?"

I looked around my familiar with a suspicious eye.

"What's wrong with you?" I asked with my finger on the manual button.

"You can move your finger. It's nothing bad. At least I don't think so." Vinnie revved his engine a couple of times before he pulled out of the parking space and out of the SKUL parking lot. "Mick came out for a little chat and I let him in."

"You what?" I gripped the wheel. "What did you say to him?"

"He certainly holds a grudge about a few things." He sounded more amused than his normal straightforward tone. "He didn't like how I took him for a little joy ride when the two of you were investigating Mystic Couture.

But I did remind him that I was the one who took the bullets for him while he was safe inside of me."

"You're right." It shouldn't have been a fond memory but it was. Granted, the situation turned out in our favor, but the look on Mick's face had been priceless. "What else did you say?" I asked wondering if Vinnie had given Mick a hard time about my feelings.

"Don't worry. I just told him that you weren't in the market for a male companion and that you were still trying to figure out your Life's Journey and if it came down to it, I'd save you over him anytime." Vinnie's engine roared down the interstate toward Belgravia Court.

"Vinnie," I groaned. "You need to keep your mouth shut."

He picked up speed.

"Vinnie." I wanted him to respond. "Vinnie."

"You asked me to keep my mouth shut." Vinnie picked up speed and shut down his circuits.

Chapter Twenty

"You made it just in time." Mom was putting the stew pot on the table just as I walked through the door.

Right next to my seat at the table was Mick Jasper.

"Agent Mick has joined us." Mom smiled and drummed her fingers together.

"Mick. Just Mick." His words were for Mom, but his eyes were focused on me.

"I see that." I put the file Burt had given me on the counter before I washed up for supper.

"You didn't know he was coming, did you?" Lilith walked over to the kitchen sink and whispered to me before she turned and rested her backside on the counter as she looked at Mom and Auntie Meme fussing all over Mick.

"No idea." I cocked a brow. "Did he show up or what?"

"Nope, Mom had called me earlier and told me to head to the coven room to grab some bat wing to put in the special stew for tonight." She crossed her arms and curled her fingers around her biceps. "That means one thing."

"What?" I asked and used the kitchen towel to dry my hands.

"They are bringing their best recipes to make a union of sorts." She shook her head. "He's a catch and they know it."

I rolled my eyes and let out a big sigh before I threw the kitchen towel on the counter and headed over to the table.

"Do you want a biscuit?" I asked Mick and held the bread basket close to my chest.

"I'd love one." He smiled that irresistible smile that was devastatingly handsome and made Mom and Auntie swoon.

"Great." I took my finger and pointed at a biscuit in the basket. Lifting my finger, I guided the biscuit over top of Mick's bowl of stew and let it drop, splattering stew all over his fancy button down.

"Oops." I grabbed my napkin and rubbed his down his shirt, trying not to picture what was under there. All I knew was I had to make it as uncomfortable for him as I could.

Mom and Auntie Meme were up to their old match-making tricks and this was not the relationship Mick and I had.

"I've got it." Mick grabbed my hand, giving it a firm squeeze, flattening it to his chest.

His heart beat thumped against my palm. Our eyes met. I caught my breath as it skipped a beat and got in time with his. It was as if time had stopped and we were the only two in the room.

"I. . .I'm sorry." I shook the spell-bound look that was not one bit a spell between us and slipped my hand from his chest.

Still looking at me, he shifted in his chair and cleared his throat. Both of us looked up at the same time. Mom and Auntie Meme were smiling and Lilith had the look of horror on her face.

"What?" I asked and shrugged, picking up my spoon to get my first taste of stew.

"Nothing," they all mumbled and went back to eating.

It crossed my mind to make the supper very uncomfortable for all of us, but I was a grown up and I needed to act like it. I could handle Mom and Auntie Meme and I certainly knew that Mick and I were only partners.

Seriously, he was just getting used to the idea that witches weren't just in books.

"Tell me about the diner." Mick looked at Auntie Meme. "I have to confess that I did a little checking around when I first met Maggie because I needed something from her and the only way to get it was to sort of blackmail her."

"Sort of?" I laughed and pulled my leg up under me in the chair as I reached across the table to grab another biscuit. "You did blackmail me saying we didn't have a real bill of sale and that there was no trail of taxes."

"Did you do a little," he wiggled his fingers at me as if he was casting a spell, "on the paperwork?"

"I did. I had to. There was no way I was going to tell you about my family. After all," I bantered back and forth with him, "I was just figuring out my Life's Journey and how could I explain it to you when I didn't understand it." I took a bite of biscuit and looked up to my family where they all looked to be entertained as Mick and I had reminisced. "It was funny."

"To you it might've been funny, but you made me feel nuts." Mick took his napkin and lifted it to my chin. "Here, you have some," he stopped talking and pointed, "here." He handed me the napkin. "You have some food on your chin."

"Thank you," I felt my face turning red as I gently took his napkin and brushed my chin with it.

Vinnie's horn beeped a few times. I ignored it. He was okay with Mick and I working as partners but certainly not as anything more than that. He beeped a few more times until he must've realized I wasn't going to come out there.

Both of us stopped talking and focused on eating our food. It didn't take but a few minutes for Lilith to fill the silence.

"So do you have any leads on who killed Angela Fritz?" she asked.

"Unfortunately, we don't. We don't even know if her murder is related to the other women." Mick rested his forearms on the edge of the table.

The sun was setting and the orange fall sky spread its light throughout the kitchen, casting a shadow on the wall.

As Mick answered or tried to answer the questions my family had for him not only about the case we were working on, but SKUL in general, a strange shadow caught my attention. It was the perfect outline of a hat. The exact same hat that the mystery person had been wearing.

I jumped up, knocking my chair to the ground just as a bullet came whizzing by my head. My necklace warmed to my chest. Auntie Meme, Mom and Lilith lifted into the air as they appeared in their coven uniform.

"It's a witch hunt!" Auntie Meme's eyes beamed a bright yellow light straight out the bullet hole that was in the window above the sink. They joined hands.

"Maggie," Mom stuck her hand out for me to take on the left and Lilith was on the right as they hovered over Mick and me.

"Come on!" I grabbed Mick by the arm. "Mom, protect the house!" I screamed on my way out the door. The gate to the back yard was open and slightly swinging as if someone had smacked it open to run out.

Vinnie was ready and waiting in the alley behind the house.

"Maggie, you need to stop." Mick looked over Vinnie's hood as he stood on the passenger side. "We need to call SKUL."

"We need to catch that person!" I slid in the driver's seat. Mick looked in the open passenger door at me. "Either you are coming or not."

"I'm coming." He jumped in and Vinnie slammed his door. "I'm going to have to get used to that."

"Hold on," Vinnie's wheels squealed. His engine roared before it died. "Maggie, I have some unfortunate news."

"We don't have time for unfortunate news. Go!" I pointed to the alley.

When nothing happened, I flipped the manual switch and tried to start Vinnie. Nothing happened. I tried a second time. Nothing.

I flipped the switch back on to Vinnie. His circuit was dim.

"Vinnie, what's happened?" I asked and punched in a few buttons.

"That person tampered with my gas tank," Vinnie's voice was faint. "I tried to warn you."

"The beeping while we were eating dinner," Mick reminded me.

My chin dropped to my chest, my hands dropped in my lap.

"I thought he was trying to stop me and you from talking. He gets jealous sometimes." My words were a mere whisper.

"We need to call Burt," Mick suggested. "We don't know if they were here to kill me or you."

"Or both." I opened the door and got out. I waited by the garage door for Mick and when he didn't get out, I peered down into the car. I tapped on his window. "You coming?"

He opened the door.

"I guess I was waiting for the door to open on its own." He got out. "But I guess if Vinnie is dead he can't open it."

"He's not dead." I corrected him. "They did something with his tank he said."

Mick and I made our way around to the gas tank. Mick bent down and smelled the tank.

"They've put sugar in it." He stood back up and put the lid back on the tank opening. "You are going to need a mechanic to flush out his system."

Those were words I didn't need to hear. The only person who could work on Vinnie was Abram Callahan and I hadn't talked to him since I cut him out of our witchy world when I put the memory spell on him after he'd kind of fallen in love with me and wanted more than I did.

At the time, Mom and Auntie Meme would've wanted me to date and marry Abram, but that was before my Life's Journey was discovered. Now they seemed to be on the Mick Jasper band wagon.

"We have to call Burt to come and make this a crime scene." Mick's words stung me to my core right as a flash of lightning crossed the sky.

"We have worked so hard to keep our identity secret." I knew that Mom and Auntie Meme were going to have a fit when Burt and the SKUL agents showed up along with the police. And I was pretty sure they were the ones who'd caused the change in the weather pattern that seemed to be developing overhead.

"I'm sorry, Maggie, but you should've thought about what it meant to be a SKUL agent when you agreed to this Life's Journey." Mick pretended to act like he knew what he was saying.

"It's not something I chose." Anger began to boil in me, as if I'd really chosen to put my family in danger. I stalked back to the house and didn't turn around when I didn't hear Mick following me.

With my hand on the handle of the back door, I glanced over my shoulder. Darkness had settled over Belgravia Court and the light of the moon dotted the ground as the leaves on the trees shifted from a howling wind. Mick was on his phone, no doubt with Burt.

"Everything needs to be in order," I instructed Mom, Lilith, and Auntie Meme when I walked in.

They were still hovering over the kitchen table with their legs crossed and holding hands in a circle.

"I said that we have to go back to normal!" I screamed at the top of my lungs.

"We are doing normal." Auntie Meme opened one eye and shifted it at me.

"I mean mortal normal," I said and waited for them to float down.

When nothing happened, I stomped my foot on the ground and clapped my hands.

"Now! The police will be here any minute. And you are right. If they see the three of you dangling in the air, then they will have a witch hunt out for us." There was no time to dilly-dally.

The three of them dropped hands, uncrossed their legs and floated down next to me.

"That person was trying to kill me or Mick." I gestured between the door and me. I looked between my two elders. "That's what happens when you go and try to play match maker with a mortal. We are not a couple. Get that through that red head of yours." I pointed directly at Auntie Meme.

She lifted her hand and pushed my finger to the side. "Don't you dare point that thing at me."

I took a step back. Even though I was in charge of my Life's Journey, Auntie Meme was not only my guardian, but she was an elder who was to be respected.

"I'm sorry, but we are not playing around here. Someone followed either myself here or Mick. They put sugar in Vinnie's tank and he is not working. Mick is out there calling SKUL who will in no time," there was a knock on the front door, "as in now, they are here."

I sucked in a deep breath. I looked between the three of them.

"Change your clothes. Be mortal normal. And you do not know that I work for SKUL. Got it?" My stern voice hopefully told them I was serious, but with these three, you never knew.

I walked down the winter wonderland hall and my gut wrenched. It took everything I had not to snap my fingers and make the old Victorian go back to no decorations, but I resisted.

"Burt, I'm so glad you are here." Burt and Sherry along with a few other agents I didn't know and a couple of police officers stood on the other side. I swung the door open for them to come on in.

"Merry Christmas?" Burt asked after he stepped in the foyer.

"Our house is entered into the Belgravia Court Historic Homes Christmas Tour and my mom wanted to get a jump on the decorating." I shut the door behind them after they all made it into the house. "Straight down the hall is the kitchen. Everyone is in there."

I followed them and noticed them looking around at the decorations. Thank goodness Mom, Lilith, and Auntie Meme were dressed in normal clothing.

"Tea anyone?" Mom turned around with a tray that had a tea pot and tea cups neatly placed on it.

"Tea cakes?" Auntie twisted behind her with a tray of pastries.

"I have nothing to offer." Lilith smiled. "I'm Maggie's sister, Lilith."

"All of you seem awfully calm for people who were just in the line of fire," Burt said, looking around.

"Take two." Auntie Meme winked at Sherry. "You could put on a couple pounds."

Sherry smiled. "I have missed your cooking."

"You can come back to work anytime." Auntie Meme had put a spell on Sherry while she worked there while I took Sherry's undercover position a couple months ago.

Auntie had made Sherry the perfect worker. She made Sherry into her mini-Meme.

"Sir." A police officer stepped inside with Mick on his heels.

Mick's eyes met mine. There was a fear in his eyes that I'd never seen before. He'd always been strong, full of confidence and a protector. That was not what I saw.

The officer handed Burt something. Burt looked at them and then walked over to me.

"I guess we know who they were here to kill." Burt handed me the photos the police officer had handed him.

As I looked at the photos taken of myself at The Brew, SKUL headquarters in the area that looked like the dental office, and The Derby.

"How on Earth have you been followed and we not know?" Auntie Meme's pleasant pastry voice had quickly been replaced by a concerned guardian.

Mom swung her arms in front of her, making everyone around us freeze. Everyone but Mick.

"Whoa," Mick's mouth dropped. "I don't think that was a good idea."

"I think it was just fine, young man." Mom darted the look to Mick. He took a step back and realized he'd be best to keep out of it.

"Young lady, this means that Vinnie didn't feel fear." Auntie Meme's eyes haunted me. "That makes me wonder if this person is someone you know. The both of you know." She wiggled a finger at me and one at Mick.

"If Vinnie knew this person and didn't feel fear, then when the person came to the house, Vinnie didn't make noise until the person started messing with his gas tank. That's why he only had time to beep a few times." I noted how Vinnie had beeped a few times while we were eating.

"Who could it be?" Lilith asked. "This is just too close to home."

"Can't you just do that snapping thing?" Mick asked.

"I told you that it didn't work that way." I knew he was having a hard time understanding the witchy ways and it was going to take time.

"We don't have the ability to know all. We are invested in our Life's Journey and sort of experts on that. Maggie found SKUL because she is good at putting basic clues together since she had a strange ability to do that, but she can't stop fate. Or just say hello, tell me who is after me." Mom did her best to explain to Mick but I could see the confusion on his face.

"This isn't like the movies. Look at it like this, we are able to do small spells on a small scale. Or things to help keep us safe in our Life's Journey. We have tools to use in our jobs like. . ." I tried to think of the right word, "An electrician. Or an officer in the army."

"But you can't figure out who was here?" he asked again.

"No." I finally had to say, "I will leave the hard investigative work to you, while I do the citizen witchy work Burt has hired me to do. Now, can you please make things go back to normal?"

Mom swept her arms around in a circle.

"Have you noticed anyone following you?" Burt asked as he came back to life, not skipping a beat from being momentarily frozen.

"No." It wasn't that I'd not noticed, it was that Vinnie hadn't warned me and I relied on him to keep me safe. I lifted my hand to my necklace. "Well," I thought back for a minute. "You know, I have seen a person with a hat and long black coat at all of those places."

"You didn't tell us?" Sherry asked.

"I didn't see why it was important to this case." I gulped. "And I saw a shadow of the hat right before the gun shots."

"Where was this shadow?" Burt asked.

"From the window." I pointed to the window over the kitchen sink.

"I mean all the places you've seen this hatted person." Burt encouraged me.

"I saw him at The Brew one morning a few days ago and before you even hired me for the job." My mouth dropped when I realized the person had following me since the other women had been killed. "And I saw the person at the St. James Art Festival after we'd just gotten done talking with Angela Fritz."

"And you were with Mick there, right?" Sherry asked.

I nodded my head. It had to be the killer.

"I'm sure if we can find the hatted person, we will have our killer." Sherry took the lead. "Think about it. Mick has been seen with Maggie on a few occasions. He's been to the diner to eat. He's been here. He was with her the day of the art festival where the person obviously checked in how Mick knew Angela. The person killed Angela while she's in town and now he's going to try to get to Maggie."

"So wherever Maggie will be, they will be trying to kill her." Mick finished Sherry's sentence making me a tad bit jealous since she was his actual partner on a regular basis and I was just on an as-needed citizen basis.

"We need to get all the video footage at The Brew." Burt turned to Auntie Meme.

"We don't have a security camera." Auntie Meme eyed Burt, knowing it was very unusual that she didn't have it since most insurance companies did require it of establishments.

"And your insurance company allows that?" Burt questioned.

"We have to look into it for our new policy," Mom said knowing that Auntie wasn't going to really understand what he was saying. "We are actually meeting with the insurance company next week to go over our policy."

"Look into surrounding businesses around The Brew as well as get footage from The Derby and ask on social media for any photos that might've been taken at the festival." The officer wrote down everything Burt was saying.

"We came as fast as our brooms could fly us." Glinda rushed through the door with the other ladies in the Spell Circle. They stopped when they noticed we had company. "Gentleman. Sherry."

"Um. . ." Sherry looked between the women dressed in their witch's clothes. "Do I know you?"

"Why, honey, we are the ones who put that. . ." Charmary started to say, but I stopped her.

"They come to the diner on a regular basis and you waited on them while I was unable to work that time a few months back." I was proud of myself for thinking quick on my feet.

"Oh yes." Sherry played off a good lie that she had no idea she was part of. She did a good job acting like she really did remember them. Only in truth, they'd put her in a levitation state and she floated above the couch for a long time. That was until Mrs. Hubbard showed up, which reminded me that Mrs. Hubbard was probably all over those binoculars in her front room trying to get a glimpse of what was going on over here.

I was a little shocked that she'd not scurried over to find out for herself.

"Sir, these are Auntie Meme's book club members." Mick did the formal introductions as Auntie beamed with pride. "They are reading *The Lion, The Witch, and The Wardrobe* for book club and they love to play the part," he whispered to Burt as if he didn't want to hurt their feelings by talking about their appearance.

"Yeah," I shrugged. "Doesn't every book club dress up?"

Burt eye-balled each of them before he went back to the investigation. "If you don't mind taking your book club somewhere else. This is the middle of a crime scene."

Auntie Meme gathered the ladies and escorted them to the basement where I was sure they were going to make a protective spell over the house.

Chapter Twenty-One

"We could've done all of that in five minutes," Glinda lifted a brow talking about the two hours that it took the police and the SKUL agents to comb the house and the back yard including Vinnie.

I was a little thankful Vinnie wasn't charged to speaking because I'm not sure he'd have been so open to people putting fingerprint powder all over his shiny coat and chrome wheel. He took pride in keeping himself clean and he was pitiful sitting in the garage.

The police had released our house back to us and it was business as usual. Mom was back to fretting over her decorations and scouring Pinterest for designs. Her problem was that she loved everything she saw and wanted to make the house look like Santa had vomited all the decorations he'd ever seen in our house in one night. I encouraged her to pick one specific theme and stick to it.

"At least we got a lot of protection spells complete for all the other covens." Flora nodded, holding on to her pointy hat as it teetered back and forth on her head.

When the Spell Circle had emerged, Mom needed their help to get her herbs together for smudge bundles for other covens as well as her herbs ready for the diner. She had them laid out all over the family room. Everyone had a hand in putting them together including the Spell Circle.

"If you'll excuse me." I stood up from the table and wondered about Mick. He said that he'd see me in the morning at The Brew for an early cup of coffee.

"Where are you going?" Lilith asked.

"I'm going to visit Mrs. Hubbard." I saw Auntie glance up at me. I'd yet to go snoop and it was time I did so. Plus,

I wanted to stop any sort of gossip that she might've concocted in her head because I'm about one hundred percent sure that there was no way she'd come up with a tale that someone had been following me and tried to kill me tonight.

"I'm going with you." Lilith jumped up and grabbed her jacket off the hook from the coat tree that Auntie Meme had also strung blue twinkle lights on. There wasn't a space in the foyer that wasn't covered in twinkle or glitter.

"We won't be long." I grabbed my coat and shut the door behind me. "She looking?" I asked as we walked across the green.

"Mmhmmm." Lilith knew that Mom was on edge.

Even though the killer was more than likely long gone, but I could tell that Mom wanted us to stay home. On a normal night, I'd probably have gone to bed or gotten a drink at The Derby with Lilith, but not tonight.

Going to see Mrs. Hubbard seemed to be uneventful and just across the green. The gas lights dotted along the walkway and lit up the green pretty well underneath the dark sky. Mom had called off Mother Nature and the rain had stopped, but the winds were still whipping letting us know that winter was on the heels of autumn.

King greeted us before we'd even made it to the door. We stepped up on the top step and Mrs. Hubbard flung her door open. Her hair was covered in a hair net that covered all the pink curlers around her head. She had on her usual black pants and a white cardigan with her pearls hung around her neck and studs stuck in her ear lobes.

"I was about to get ready for bed." She looked between Lilith and me. There were perfect circles around her eyes that just so happened to be the same sized circles on the lens of binoculars. "But I guess you can come in for a bit of cake."

"That sounds wonderful." I pushed her door open and Lilith wiggled her nose just as King lunged at my ankles.

He squealed and ran back toward Mrs. Hubbard's kitchen.

"I don't know what it is about you two, but he is scared to death of you." Mrs. Hubbard motioned for us to come in before she took off after him. "King, baby. Come to Mommy."

"Look." I pointed to the binoculars Mrs. Hubbard kept next to the chair positioned right in front of her window that had a perfect view of our house. "She sits here all day long and watches everything we do."

"Girls," Mrs. Hubbard called. "Why don't you come in here because there's not enough room for us in there."

Lilith glared and pointed, looking down her finger like she was looking down a gun. "It takes every inch in my witch finger not to cast a spell on her that even Auntie Meme would be mad at me for."

"Stop." I pushed her hand down to her side. "She's an old lady. Now you see why I had suggested her cakes for the diner. It keeps her out of Mom's hair and sight, but now she'd done messed that up."

"Coming!" Lilith called and motioned for me to go ahead of her.

The kitchen smelled so good. Her little cakes were cooling on a cooling rack. I couldn't help but notice a few of them were burnt. Nothing like the ones she'd made for me a couple of months ago and far from the ones she'd made at The Brew.

"That's a lot of cakes for a late night." I sat down at the small café table in her kitchen. I reached for the plate she'd put in the middle of the table, but noticed the sides of them were burnt where there wasn't icing.

"My house is falling apart." She sat down. Her lips frowned. "I can deal with the faucets dripping, the water leak that made my ceiling in my bedroom fall, and the dishwasher is broken, but my stove." She shook her head. Sadness crept up into her eyes. "I don't know what I'm going to do if I can't get that fixed."

"I'm so sorry the cakes didn't work out at the diner." I felt a little responsible now that I new she really needed the money.

"It's fine. I'm old and not many people want to hire me, but I guess I could go to that big box store and be a greeter." She leaned over and rubbed her ankle. "I'm not sure how my feet will hold up, but I bet it will help pay for rent."

"Rent?" I asked.

"Yes. I'm afraid I'm going to have to move off of Belgravia Court." She sighed; her head fell to her chest.

Lilith and I looked at each other. There was no way I could ask about Joe. I didn't want to make her sadder than she already was since I knew the date hadn't turned out the way she'd hoped. At least that was according to Joe.

"Where is Brian?" Lilith asked.

I looked at Lilith and mouthed, "What?"

"Why on Earth would you ask about Brian?" I whispered in fear Mrs. Hubbard was going to bring up his drunken escapade.

"Now that your family is the talk of the court with all that police ruckus over there, they've all forgotten about how one of you got him drunk." Her eyes dragged back and forth between Lilith and me. "But I'm going to put that behind me and enjoy him for the next few days until he has to go back to the city."

She stood back up and walked over to her counter where she retrieved a stack full of sketchpads and set them on the table.

"He's such a good artist. I tried to tell him that he needed to do art and not worry with all the gallery stuff." She flipped pages of a sketchbook.

"You know that nothing was going on at our house." Lilith had decided to get the rumors stopped that I'm sure Mrs. Hubbard had already started about the police.

"I wasn't going to say anything." Mrs. Hubbard wrinkled her forehead and put her teacup up to her lips.

Sure you weren't, my mind said as my hand dragged one of the sketchpads across the table. I'd better occupy myself with Brian's sketches so my lips wouldn't get me in trouble.

"No, really. Mom has been dating this cop and they were over helping her get a huge Christmas tree out of the attic, that's all," Lilith lied. "You know Mom, she is bound and determined to win the Christmas tour first place."

Lilith had struck a cord with Mrs. Hubbard. She was always trying to win every single competition Belgravia Court participated in. But with the unfortunate events of the status of her house and income, it looked like there was no way she'd be participating this year.

The two of them bantered back and forth and my fingers kept swiping the pages. Mrs. Hubbard was right. Brian was a fantastic artist and it did seem a shame that he wasted his talents seeking out other artists' work to display when he should've been displaying his own.

My mind skidded to a stop as my eyes scanned the two-page sketch layout. It was a pencil design that I was positive I'd seen somewhere else. There was something written very small in the corner of the page. I focused on those words and used a little bit of magic to enlarge them.

"*The Ville*?" I gasped. Blood pulsed through my veins as I tried to suck air into my lungs. "Franklin?"

"Huh?" Lilith glanced my way. "Are you okay?"

I swung the book around to Mrs. Hubbard. "Mrs. Hubbard?" I jabbed the picture. "Who is Franklin?"

"My nephew." She looked at me funny and drew back. "Well," she let out a chuckle, "his real name is Franklin Bingo and he hated that name. So when he went to New York after high school, he decided to change his name to Brian Mingo. You know artists."

"Where did he go to high school?" I asked.

"Louisville High of course." She confirmed my worst fear. "His parents insisted he go there."

"Do you happen to know when he graduated?" I asked, and when she told me the exact same year that Mick Jasper, Angela Fritz, and Big Stevenson had graduated, my gut churned. "And do you know where he is right now?" I closed my eyes.

"He said he was going to see an old friend at the Galt House and would be back later." She tilted her head. "Why?"

"I've got to go. I'll see you later, Lilith." I grabbed the sketchbook and didn't wait for her to stop me. I hoped I wasn't too late to save Georgette because I was one-hundred-percent positive that was Franklin's next move.

I just couldn't believe it. This entire time the killer was right across the green from me and I had no idea. It all made sense to me. Angela Fritz had stolen his design and I'm not sure how, but it was his revenge.

As fast as I could, I ran across the green to grab whatever transportation necessary to get me to the Galt House.

"Mom!" I screamed as soon as I slammed the door behind me. I looked in the family room but all the herbs had been cleaned up and the snowmen were all lit up and smiling. "Auntie Meme!" I yelled running through winter wonderland and into the kitchen.

The back door was open and the outside twinkling lights Mom had strung across our outdoor living space and around the pool were swaying in the cool breeze. The sound of laughter that trickled through the sound of the rustlings leaves seemed to be coming from the garage.

"Mom?" I headed through her herb garden and out the gate to the garage where the Spell Circle had gathered around Vinnie and were drinking bubbling brew that I was sure they'd whipped up from a potion. "What is going on?" I asked and looked at the cups they were holding.

"You are not going to believe this," Mom spoke with delight. "Our very own Flora knows how to work on cars. Her father was a mechanic."

"This means that I'll have Vinnie fixed up in no time." Flora's brown hair stuck up even more as she ran her hand down the side of Vinnie.

It was as if she'd put her head in an electric socket, only her hair did that most of the time anyway, it was just extra tonight. She circled the car a few times, keeping her hand on it the entire time. The more she went around Vinnie, the quicker her steps became. On her last lap, she grabbed Mom's cup and when she made it to the gas tank, she poured the contents of Mom's bubbling drink into the tank. Flora used her hand to rub into Vinnie's panel the drips that didn't make it into the tank. She did another lap and grabbed Charmary's cup and repeated exactly what she'd done with Mom's. She continued this process until all the cups of bubbling brew were inside of Vinnie's tank.

A couple of times I tried to protest that Vinnie wouldn't like the mess and tried to ask Mom permission to use her broom for an emergency fly, but was greeted with hushes and shushing.

"That was not fun, Maggie Park." Vinnie's lights blinked on.

Everyone, including myself, jumped with joy.

"We've got to go." It was like Vinnie hadn't skipped a beat. The driver's side door opened, I gave Flora a big hug and kiss on the cheek before I got in the car.

"I'm so sorry," I said to Vinnie as soon as he pulled out of the alley. "But I need you to take me to the Galt House as fast as you can. I'm going to make Franklin Bingo pay for not only what he did to those women, but what he did to you."

"Thank you, Maggie. I think I tried to warn you." Vinnie sounded a little vague. "At least I feel like I did. I am still a little bit groggy but I will be fine as soon as I get my pistons greased and that slop off the side of my car."

"You did great. I'm sure you'll be feeling back to old Vinnie in no time." I assured him.

The air inside of me and the air in Vinnie was tense. I'd forgotten my cell phone on the counter in the kitchen.

"I need you to go get Mick as soon as you drop me off and bring him to the Galt House. Understand?" I asked Vinnie since he didn't seem to be on top of his game just yet.

"Yes, Maggie. You listen to your necklace." Vinnie skidded to a stop in front of the Galt House and opened the door.

"Listen?" I asked.

"Yes, Flora put in the new voice system when she fixed me. This allows you and me to communicate through voice instead of feeling." That was going to make it a lot easier on me and quicker when I needed him.

"I'll talk if I need you." I jumped out of the car with the sketchbook in my hand and didn't look back.

There must've been a big event happening at the hotel. There were ladies dressed in formals and men dressed in tuxedos.

I headed straight for the elevator fully prepared to do whatever magic I needed to do to get to the penthouse.

"Maggie?" The voice caught me by surprise.

"Mick," I stood in shock that he was here and with a beautiful brunette on his arm whose royal blue sequin gown clung to her skin showing off a killer body underneath. "What are you doing here?"

"Dr. Artie's retirement party is tonight, but he's technically not retiring until January first." He kept his eyes on me. I kept my eyes on her. "This is Lori Littleman, Dr. Artie's daughter."

"Nice to meet you." I threw a grin on my face knowing that Brian was upstairs this very minute trying to kill Georgette, unless he already had. "Can I speak with you for a minute?"

"Lori. Mick," Dr. Artie called from the entrance of the grand ballroom. We all looked at him and he waved them to come on.

"It's time." Lori patted Mick's arm. "If you'll excuse us. We are introducing Daddy to the party goers."

"I'm sorry." My head ducked front and back as I tugged on Mick's coat. "I just need him for a tiny second."

"Hurry up," Mick pulled me out of earshot of Lori.

"You can't go in there. I need you." My heart was beating so hard I felt like it was going to pop right out of my chest. "Brian Mingo is really a guy you went to school with. Franklin Bingo. Do you remember him?"

"No." Mick shook his head.

"Here." I shoved the open sketchbook in his face. I looked over at Dr. Artie who was checking his watch and tapping the toe of his fancy shoe waiting for Mick. "You met him the other night at The Derby when you were there with me and Lilith. He's Mrs. Hubbard's nephew. Don't you remember?"

"You know; I remember seeing him but I didn't pay too much attention." He shut the book and handed it to me.

"Anyways, long story short," I had no time to tell him how I got the sketch book, "Mrs. Hubbard said that he was here to say goodbye to friend before he headed back to the city. Georgette is up there with the actual painting. Didn't you say that Angela was having you look into Franklin Bingo?"

"He went to school with us." He snapped his fingers. "You know that picture you put on the dart board at The Derby?" I nodded. "That other kid in the background was Franklin. I remember that he had a huge crush on Angela and she didn't give him the time of day. One day," it was as if Mick was putting together the clues as to why Mick was being targeted and anyone associated with him was being murdered, "she had me say something to the kid because he'd been stalking her and drawing all sorts of strange pictures."

"But how did she get his design and why would she call it her own?" I questioned.

"Only one way to find out." Mick jabbed the up elevator button and the door slid open.

"Mick!" Dr. Artie yelled as we started to step inside. "Where are you going?" He hurried over to the elevator and put his hand on the door to stop it from closing.

"You're going to have to start without me," Mick said. "I've got a job to do."

"You are on leave and I'm not sure your mental health is up to it." Dr. Artie didn't worry about what his guests would think. "I think you need to come on in and tell Burt whatever it is that's going on."

"I don't have time," Mick looked at me and I touched the penthouse button with a little magic so it would light up since we didn't have the penthouse access key.

"Then I'm going with you. I'm not going to let you destroy yourself." Dr. Artie jumped into the elevator.

The closer we got to the penthouse, the hotter my necklace got warning me of danger. I rubbed my finger across it so Vinnie knew I was okay and recognized the alert. Mick watched as I did my witch thing, realizing that I had been communicating with Vinnie.

"Damn, I wish I had my gun." Mick stared at the floor levels as they lit up. When we hit the penthouse, he looked at me and sighed, "You ready?'

"Yes." I jumped out of the elevator door with Mick and Dr. Artie behind me. I knew that I was going to have to erase any witchy things Dr. Artie might see me do but Mick and I certainly could use the backup.

The door to Angela's penthouse was slightly open. I pushed it with the toe of my shoe and looked inside.

"Georgette?" I called. When I didn't hear a response, I walked a little deeper into the penthouse. "Brian, it's Maggie Park, your aunt's neighbor. Are you here?"

"Look around," Mick said when we noticed the paper on *The Ville* painting had been ripped open and the painting was exposed. "Be careful."

Mick picked up a candlestick from the side table next to the couch and held it like a weapon. He went in the opposite direction as me and Dr. Artie seemed to stay frozen at the door.

I walked into the bedroom and it looked like Georgette had been packing the suitcase that was lying on top of the bed. Next to the bed, lying on the floor was the black hat. A shifting noise barely sounded in my ear. I pushed open the bathroom door. The curtain on the bathtub was closed, but swaying.

"Are you in here, Brian?" I asked and took another step closer to the tub. I gripped the edge of the shower curtain and ripped it open.

Georgette and Brian were gagged and bound to each other. Both bright eyed and frightened. Brian had on the black coat.

"Oh my gosh," I gasped. "How did you get tied up if you were here to kill her?" I asked, circling a finger around Georgette, untying her.

She grabbed the edges of the gag and pulled it down and over her chin.

"I don't know how you did that, but get me out of here." She jumped up and immediately turned to Brian to help him.

"Wait." I tried to stop her. "Isn't he a bad guy?"

"No." She jerked the gag out of his mouth.

"I just want what is mine. *The Ville*." Brian pleaded, "Get us out of here before he comes back to finish the job like he promised."

"But you've been following me around with that hat and coat." I pointed out.

"I have because I was trying to find out where Angela was staying. I came to the diner to see my aunt Gladys that morning, but then I met you that night when I went to talk to Angela. She was talking to you. I figured you knew her and she refused to tell me where she was staying and had instructed her people to keep me at a distance." He stood up.

There was no more time for a question and answer session. The actual killer had been here and we had to find them.

After we got Brian untied and while on our way out of the bathroom, I blew a little hot air out of my mouth, dragging my chin up and down to let the erasing spell seep into their entire bodies. They only needed to remember that I saved them, not how it was done.

"Mick, why are you just sitting?" I asked with dismay when I saw him just sitting on the couch like it was no big deal there was a killer on the loose.

"Because I told him to." Dr. Artie stood in the bar area of the room fixing himself a cocktail. There was a gun lying next to the ice bucket. "I really didn't want to kill him this way, but I guess I'm going to have to."

"That's the man that killed Angela," Georgette cried out and buried herself in Brian's arms.

"He's the one who tied us up and said he'd be back to kill us." Brian hugged Georgette to his chest.

"I guess I don't know what's going on." I looked around the room. I thought for sure Brian was the killer. It had all added up. My necklace warmed. "A little too late," I whispered hoping that Vinnie would hear me if it was true what he'd said about the voice thing.

"I have no idea what SKUL was thinking when they hired you. I knew Burt was an idiot, but when he proposed that he hire a citizen who could fit in, it just made him downright a fool," Dr. Artie scoffed. "You see," he picked up the gun and motioned for Georgette, Brian, and me to join Mick on the couch and we did. "I've been waiting all these years for the perfect time to kill the women in Mick's life and make him feel the pain I have felt. I'd waited patiently for him to get married and have children so I could do to him what he did to my precious Marjorie."

"Your precious Marjorie?" I asked. "As in Steepleton?"

"She and Lori were all I had from my beloved Irene," Artie began to tell his story, "who died of cancer. Irene was a very independent woman and I loved that about her. She kept her name when we married and agreed we'd have two children. One bearing each of our surnames. Since Marjorie was our first and was a girl, Irene insisted she have her last name. When our second child, Lori was born, we gave her my name. Then you." He jabbed the gun toward Mick. "It was your responsibility to keep her safe."

"This explains why I'm not getting any help seeing you," Mick muttered. "You've been sabotaging our appointments for years. I knew I wasn't crazy, you just made me feel like it."

"Initially I wanted to make you go crazy and be admitted for the rest of your life, but you fought me the whole way. It was then that I thought I'd wait you out and kill your child as you did mine, but you seem to pride yourself on being a bachelor. It was easy to find all the women you had loved and left through our sessions. You rambled on and on and I kept every single detail about them. But you." He slid the barrel of the gun at me. "You seem to have a special place in his heart, so I knew that I would have to have to perfect opportunity to kill you. When I followed you home and Mick just so happened to be there, I knew it was going to be perfect to kill you right in front of him."

The evil words dripped out of his mouth and onto each of us. He made my skin crawl with fear.

"Can you just let me go?" Brian spoke up. "I won't breathe a word of this to anyone and you can keep the painting."

"Shut up!" Dr. Artie yelled. "You are the killer." A deep laugh escaped Dr. Artie's mouth. "Can't you see? It's perfect. Mick told me all about your little argument growing up years ago when we first revisited his past. I kept very detailed notes. When he said that his longtime friend and famous artist Angela Fritz was coming to town, I knew it was then that I had to plan the murders because he'd been trying to help her solve the little tiff you, Franklin Bingo, were having with her. When I did a little digging around and found out that you were Brian Mingo, it all fit together like a nice little puzzle."

"A little too nice," Burt's voice boomed out from behind his. "Drop the gun, Artie. You are surrounded and we have every word you said on tape."

Artie stood there with the gun pointed as if he had options to weigh.

"Daddy, please. Please drop the gun," a heartbroken Lori pleaded behind Burt.

It was as if something snapped deep inside of Artie. His grip on the gun opened, dropping the weapon to the floor. Mick scrambled to get it and once he had it he pointed it at Artie. Lori came rushing to his side, taking her distraught father into her arms before the SKUL agents zeroed in on them, hauling Artie out of the room.

Chapter Twenty-Two

"I have to admit that I didn't think you were going to be able to get it done." I stood in Mrs. Hubbard's kitchen and checked out the newly remodeled room that was going to be perfect for Mrs. Hubbard to make her cakes. "You did a great job." I nudged Brian with my elbow. "Maybe you should think about going into carpentry instead of painting."

"No way. I can't wait to get back to work." He stood in the middle of the kitchen admiring his handiwork. "This was sort of like artistry work to me. It was fun fitting in all the pieces and doing it in a way that was functional for my aunt. Now that I have the money from the sale of *The Ville* and the back money that Angela had been paid for it, I'm happy to have helped my aunt out by fixing everything that wasn't working."

"Plus she got that deal with that bakery too, so she'll be able to have even more money." I helped him move some of the kitchen furniture back in place.

"If it weren't for you and your aunt giving her that little time to make her cakes at the diner, the bakery owner never would've ordered one." Brian smiled.

"So, I guess you are for sure leaving right after supper?" I asked.

"I really wanted to leave before now, but I do have so much to be thankful for and since your family offered to host us for Thanksgiving, I knew I could extend my stay," he said. "Plus, your sister said she'd take me to The Derby. Maybe this time I can get her drunk."

"Don't count on it." I laughed. "I'm going to head on over to the house and check on the turkey. I'll see you and Mrs. Hubbard soon."

I headed out the front door and across the green. The sky had turned grey and there were some rumblings on the news that there could possibly be a flurry or two later in the evening which just might put my mom in the Christmas spirit she still hadn't seemed to find after all these weeks of trying to get the house decorated in time for the Belgravia Court Historic Homes Christmas Tour, which would start next weekend.

The house smelled delightful. Auntie Meme had been cooking all day long, granted it was her witch way of cooking and she probably put fake scents around the house, but it still smelled like Thanksgiving.

"How is it going?" I asked Mom and Auntie Meme when I walked into the kitchen.

"It's going good," Mom nodded. "Can you go outside and help your sister get the table set. Our guest should be arriving any minute."

"Guests?" I questioned with a chuckle. "That's a little formal for Mrs. Hubbard and Brian."

Mom gave me the look and I did what she asked. Riule and Miss Kitty were outside watching as Lilith and Gilbert hurried underneath the white tent that Mom said she'd rented when in reality, she'd snapped. Lilith was arranging the place settings of white china while Gilbert flew overhead dropping a perfectly folded cloth napkin in the shape of a turkey on each plate.

"Me, you, Mom, Auntie Meme, Mrs. Hubbard, Brian," I said out loud as I counted the seats. "Who's the extra place setting for?"

"I'm assuming that's for me." Mick Jasper entered the tent with a bouquet of fall daisies in his hand and a pumpkin pie in the other. "I had come by The Brew yesterday to wish you a Happy Thanksgiving. Your auntie asked me over for dinner after I told her that I wasn't going anywhere since I was working a new case."

"Oh." I tried to conceal how happy I was to see him. We hadn't seen each other since we'd given our statements about the night we discovered Dr. Artie was the killer. "You're more than welcome."

"Then you can help finish setting the table so Gilbert can go away before the neighbors get here." Lilith sent Gilbert and the other familiars off so our nosy neighbor wouldn't be asking any unwanted questions.

Mrs. Hubbard had already been on the lookout for Miss Kitty since she was a rare owl species and the paper was offering money for any additional pictures of her—

Mrs. Cartmell had taken pictures of Miss Kitty a few months ago and leaked them to the paper. Now not just Mrs. Hubbard, but also the entire Louisville population was on the hunt for the rare bird that wasn't native to the United States. Just another reason for Auntie Meme to have a feather in her craw about Mrs. Hubbard. But today was Thanksgiving and I'd hoped Auntie could put all that behind her for just the day.

In no time, the table under the tent was filled with food, people around it, and the sounds of laughter of family and friends. It was the first time that I'd ever recalled a mortal Thanksgiving where we actually did the mortal traditional turkey supper. It was as if our witch heritage didn't exist for that moment. Even Auntie Meme and Mrs. Hubbard had made peace for the moment and exchanged a few recipes. Which I knew were all made up in Auntie's head but they sure did sound good.

All the happy, thankful merriment was getting to me. I grabbed a couple of empty plates and excused myself to put them in the kitchen while I gathered my wits. It wasn't that I wasn't happy, I was happy. But my Life's Journey sure wasn't what I thought it was going to be. Working with SKUL was my happiest, but it seemed that those opportunities were few and far between. Burt only called when he needed me to be a blend in citizen and it was the only time that I talked to or saw Mick. I hadn't heard a peep out of SKUL since the day I'd gone down and given my statement to them about Dr. Artie. They'd even kept Mick and me away from each other.

Mick hadn't tried to reach out to me, so I let it go. Seeing him tonight, for the first time in a couple weeks, really threw me off.

"Are you getting dessert?" Mick walked into the kitchen just as I had wiggled my nose at the dirty dishes and magically made them clean.

"Oh." I jumped around. "I didn't see you standing there. I guess I shouldn't have done that. Don't tell Mom, she doesn't like the whole lazy magic way out."

"Trust me." Mick dragged his finger across the whipped cream on the pumpkin pie and stuck it in his mouth. "If I could do dishes by wiggling my nose, I would." He pretended to wiggle his nose like a bunny rabbit.

I laughed, swiping my finger across the whip cream and dotted his nose with it.

"Hey." He grabbed me around my waist and dragged me to him with one arm as his other hand took a big swipe through the whip cream. After he pulled me close, his fingers wiped the cream over my mouth and chin.

I tried to move my head side-to-side.

"You deserved that." His breath prickled the skin on my neck. His broad shoulders heaved as he breathed. His clean and manly scent was better than any happy potion I'd ever had.

My heart hammered in my ears as I felt his gaze unlock something inside my soul. His gaze fell to the whip cream that he had spread across my lips, sending a tingling in the pit of my stomach. His lips lowered to where his eyes were looking. His kiss sang through my veins. It was then that I closed my eyes and saw my destiny and Life's Journey become one.

THE END

Keep reading for an excerpt of Spies and Spells and how Mick and Maggie became crime fighting partners.

Chapter One excerpt of Spies and Spells

Rowl! The soft, pink paw tapped my nose a couple of times before the old cat gave me the ole one-two punch. His midnight fur helped him blend in with the unlit room.

"Stop, Riule," I groaned, batting my mom's familiar feline away from me and jerked the pillow over my head. "Tell her I'm up." My voice muffled from underneath the pillow.

Rowl! The damn cat took a couple of more swipes at my hands gripping the pillow across my face.

I took the pillow off my face and sucked in a deep breath when I heard the paws of Riule's feet dance across my bedroom hardwood floors and out the door. Outside, the early morning breeze caused the leaves on the tree beyond my window to move around, directing the sun's rays to trickle through my blinds and dancing along my ceiling. It was a habitual morning dance between the two, which let me know I was going to be late for work if I didn't get my lazy hinny out of bed.

Same shit. Day in, day out. I got up, got ready, went to work, came home, ate dinner, and went to bed. Sometimes that routine included a social visit with Lilith, my sister, but definitely not a regular basis, as she too had the same schedule as me. Only she got up a couple hours earlier to go to work. Lilith worked the early shift at The Brew, our family diner that was only open for breakfast and lunch.

At twenty-eight, I still hadn't found my life's journey. No. We, my family, did not call it our ambition in life. In fact, we didn't grow up like mortal children, going to school and figuring out that we wanted to be: a teacher, doctor, lawyer or whatever. We had what was called the Witchy Hour. It was the hour on which we stumbled into our life's journey.

There wasn't much I could say about the Witchy Hour, because I had not had mine, therefore, I got up every morning and worked at the diner. Clearing dishes, taking orders and delivering food could not be my journey. I knew it in my soul.

My family was witches. Modern day, every day, normal looking kind of people. Only witches. Witches who made sure we blended into the area where we lived.

Historic Old Louisville, Kentucky, on Belgravia Court to be exact. The area was a very artsy area where a lot of hipsters hung out in the local eateries and bars.

The city was not too big or too small, allowing us to more easily fit in. And so, at age twenty-eight, I worked in our family's dinner, The Brew, until I was hit with my life's journey.

I had heard, as well as seen, witches in their journey. Take my mother, for instance, who Lilith and I still lived with along with my Great Auntie Meme along with all of our familiars. Yes, witches did have familiars. Only mine happened to be my car, Vinnie. Riule, the ornery cat, happens to be my mother's, who, by the way, was doing her dirty work this morning. Gilbert, the macaw, was Lilith's familiar and Ms. Kitty, an owl, was Auntie's.

I was the only one with a non-animal familiar, which spoke volumes to how I had led my life. I had been on a mission to find my life's journey. My job. And get out from underneath my family's home.

At times I had even wondered if Mom or Auntie Meme had put a spell on me so I would not find my journey, and so they'd have to keep me here. On Belgravia Court.

I pushed back my long black hair away from my eyes, peeling a few strands away from my cheek where it had been glued from nighttime drool, something I wasn't proud of, and pushed the quilt off me. If I didn't make some sort of movement, the one-hundred-year-old historic home wouldn't creak from under my feet and Riule would be sent back up to see what I was up to. Then smugly running back downstairs to Mom, giving her the lowdown on my laziness. They didn't realize that if I had my life's journey, I would be happy to get up every morning and go do it, just like Mom and Auntie Meme.

"What to wear?" I asked.

Growls and barks were coming from outside my front bedroom window. I made my way over and pulled back the curtain to see what all of the ruckus was about, hoping Riule hadn't gotten Mrs. Hubbard's yappy dog all stirred up.

Mrs. Hubbard was the old lady who lived in the house across from us. She bent over her flower boxes that were sitting on the brick ledge of her front porch fussing with her plastic Patagonia flower she had wired together with bread ties. She had one end of the plastic bouquet while King, the yappy Yorkie, had the other end in his mouth. King looked like he was playing. Mrs. Hubbard looked like she was not. The two played tug-of-war until King won out, rushing off the porch and under her row of hedges that lined the front of her home.

Mrs. Hubbard stood five foot with grey hair that hung down past her ears, parted to the left side, with side bangs. Mrs. Hubbard was never without her pearl earrings, pearl necklace and a cardigan. She must've had stock in pleated black slacks because it was the only color, or style, of pants she ever wore. Today her choice of cardigan happened to be hot pink, making her crazy stand out even more.

As though she knew I was watching her, she looked up and gave a slight wave. I waved back, but not quick enough to pull back and avoid her gesture to have me open my window.

"Good morning, Mrs. Hubbard." I tried to be as pleasant as I could at seven in the morning. I pushed a loose strand of hair behind my ear. "How are you?"

Ruf, ruf, ruf. King had emerged from the hedges and went from attacking the flowers to attacking the air and space between the two of us. I glared at the scrawny, wiry spit fire wondering if I could just send him up in flames, right there in front of Mrs. Hubbard. No one on Belgravia Court liked the yappy dog.

"Fair to middlin'. Fair to middlin'," she repeated shaking her head and pointing at the fake garden. "I'm trying to bring home the blue." Her eyes slid over to the front of our home where Mom took a lot of pride in her landscape and gardening.

The blue Mrs. Hubbard referred to was the annual Historic Old Louisville Hidden Treasure Garden Tour that was taken very seriously by the residents on Belgravia Court. Mrs. Hubbard being one of them. Little did they know Mom was a witch and her specialty was all things earth. She was kind of like Mother Nature, only in witch form and she also grew the best herbs for potions, which Auntie Meme liked to use on customers at The Brew.

"I need another bread tie. It looks like the coons got my flowers. I'm going to give those coons a knuckle sandwich," Mrs. Hubbard said in a silvery tone. She shook her thin fist in the air.

I smiled. Mrs. Hubbard was the queen of what I called southernisms. Most of the time I didn't even understand what she was talking about. I wanted to tell her she wasn't going to bring home the blue with plastic flowers but there was no telling her that unless I wanted a good cussing.

"You know." She squinted up at my window. "I've never seen y'all have any sort of rodents over there." Her brows furrowed. "What's your secret?"

And there she went.

Mrs. Hubbard was nosy and she and Auntie Meme had had a few words right there in the courtyard in front of everyone. Auntie Meme told her to mind her own business, only her exact words were *my business isn't your business and unless you're my panties don't be up my ass.*

Mrs. Hubbard was as mad as a wet hen but it didn't stop her from still being nosy.

"There's no secret." There was. Auntie Meme put a rodent spell on Mrs. Hubbard's house sending every rodent on Belgravia Court over there. The Orkin man was a fixture over there.

Susie Brown, our other neighbor and Belgravia Court's neighborhood watch president, even started a rumor that Mrs. Hubbard and the Orkin man were having a fling. Only we knew the truth and we never gave into gossip. In fact, the women loved to meet up in the courtyard on Saturday nights with their fancy cocktails and catch up on the gossip on Belgravia Court. The Park family—my family—were always a topic of interest because we spent much of our time to ourselves. Well, not Auntie Meme. She spent a lot of time looking out the front window wondering what type of spell she could send Mrs. Hubbard's way. When she'd get down to the nitty-gritty of a spell, Mom wouldn't let her send it. Auntie Meme fussed that Mom let her make the spell, why not let her send it. Mom let Auntie Meme concoct the spells so she wouldn't have to entertain my feisty auntie.

Still, the neighbors loved to gossip about us. Much was speculation, but still, they lived on speculation.

"I'm getting ready to go to work. I'll see if we have any bread ties." I politely waved, pushing the window back down. I pulled the cord of the blinds, zipping them up to the top of the window to let the sunlight fully in.

I stomped over to my closet for good measure in case Mom was listening and opened the dark wood door. Everything in the house was dark and old. It was one of the things that drew Mom and Auntie to the Historic Old Louisville. The small suburb within the city held many secrets, like our family. It was old, like our family, and held comfort for Mom.

From what Mom had told me and I had gathered, when we moved to Kentucky before I was born, the family started to become more and more engrained with mortals. We were a dying breed and it was fine with me since they never let me use the magic I held inside.

Don't put a spell on that. Clean the dishes, not with a swipe of your finger. Use the laundry machines, not a wave of your hand.

But today I was going to be late and a wave of my hand might be what saved me from doing the dishes, the mortal way, in the diner.

Just like that, I raised my arm, twirling my wrist three times ending in a snap. And just like that, I was dressed in a black long-sleeved turtleneck, black skinny jeans, and a pair of cheetah print loafers. My long black hair neatly slicked back into a ponytail and minimal makeup was perfect for the home-cooked meals I'd be serving.

"Good morning." I greeted my mom who was standing at the kitchen sink window picking some basil off the potted plant. I put my hands on both of her arms, giving her a little squeeze. "Thank you for sending in Riule," my tone was sarcastic.

Riule was sitting underneath the kitchen table with his leg thrown up in the air looking like the cover model on *Cat Fancy* magazine, his tongue stopped in mid-lick as his eyes bore into mine stopping for a second and then returning to cleaning himself.

"It won't be a good morning, good afternoon, or good night if you don't get to work." Mom's eyes drew down on me. Her beautiful good looks caught me off guard. Her hair was long and black like mine. We had the same almond-shaped black eyes and oval face. She had high cheekbones like Lilith, while I had round ones that made me look younger than I really was. "Auntie Meme will work on a spell for you instead of Mrs. Hubbard."

Many times Mom and I had been in public when people had mistaken her for my sister.

"And," her eyes slid down to my toes and up to my head. Her eyes stared at me. She had crow's feet—the only facial sign she was older than me. "It seems like you got ready awfully fast." Her cool tone was filled with *I know you used magic*.

"Do we have any bread ties?" I grabbed the piece of wheat toast Mom had sitting on the counter. I closed my eyes and savored the first bite. She made the best buttered toast. There wasn't a single grain left unbuttered. Mom made sure she spread the pat of butter to the edges, letting it seep in the warm toast.

"Mrs. Hubbard?" Mom picked a few more leaves from the window garden and bundled them with a piece of cord she had already precut.

"Yes," I mumbled, stuffing the rest of the toast in my mouth.

"In the drawer." Mom waved her hand in a circular motion before uncurling her long lean finger toward the junk drawer.

"In the drawer huh?" I questioned, pulling the junk drawer open knowing it was stuffed with pens, coupon circulars, and everything but bread ties. "Talk about magic." I swiveled my eyes Mom's way, questioning her little bit of magic. "And you accuse me of using magic."

I grabbed a fistful of ties, kissed my mom on the cheek and headed out of the kitchen toward the front of the house.

"I'll be right back," I called over my shoulder and walked down the hallway, opening up the heavy wooden door to the courtyard.

Belgravia Court was an odd place to live. There were two rows of houses opposite each other with a grassy courtyard down the middle. The front of the houses faced the courtyard. Each side had its own sidewalk with gas carriage lanterns lighting the way. Along the backs of our homes was an alley with each home having a detached garage.

The houses were so close together, I couldn't spit out my side bedroom window without hitting the neighbor's house.

Belgravia Court was a close-knit community with everyone in everyone else's business. Not the Parks. We tried to stay on the down-low as much as possible. Given our heritage and all.

"I found some." I waved my fistful of bread ties in the air toward Mrs. Hubbard.

I glanced up at the sky. It was unseasonably cool for a June day in Kentucky.

Ruff, ruff, ruff. King charged me. I flicked my hand, sending a little jolt of *don't screw with me* at him. Enough for him to feel it, but not enough to hurt him. I had to keep the ankle biter from sinking his sharp little daggers in me.

King yelped, running back under the bushes.

"He has that same reaction with your crazy aunt." Mrs. Hubbard eased down her front steps and bent down to get her dog from the hedges. Her butt stuck straight up in the air, she dug her arms deeper into the bushes until she came out with a shaking King. "Oh stop that." She snuggled him against her. "Maggie isn't anything like the rest of 'em."

"They aren't so bad." I glared at the dog, holding the ties out for her to take.

"Thank you, honey." Mrs. Hubbard nodded her head to put them down on the step, glancing sideways at me. She walked back up her steps and put King in the house. She turned and said, "Tell me." She went back to the fake flowers, quickly tying some together before sticking them back in the planter boxes. "What was your mom doing up there on the balcony?"

I looked over at my house. The red three-story home was beautiful with the double porches on the front of the left side of the house. On the right were two large windows on each level. But the porches were really the charming feature. The first one was considered the front porch. Two dark grey pillars were built on the brick wall to the open porch leading up to the large wooden door with long skinny decorative windows on each side. Above the door was a stained glass window Auntie Meme had created herself. If you were to look closely, you'd see little images of our heritage.

Above the porch was another open porch with wrought iron railing. The doors leading into the house from the second porch were all glass. The room off the second porch was Mom's room. Then the third floor was where Lilith and my rooms were located. We had the whole Jack and Jill bathroom thing going. It was cute when we were kids, not so much now.

"She was doing her morning yoga." I smiled, lying.

Mom used the morning sun to welcome the day, sending a little prayer of protection for the family every morning. Normally she was careful of watchful eyes at four-thirty in the morning, and normally Mrs. Hubbard wasn't up that early. Something told me today was going to be anything but normal.

Mrs. Hubbard harrumphed, not fully satisfied with my answer, but she didn't balk at it either.

"I don't have a horse in that race. But it seems to me she'd go to one of them fancy yoga studios." Mrs. Hubbard eyed me, setting her jaw. We stood there for a second before she waved it off. She bent down and picked up a bouquet of plastic flowers. "No horse in that race."

"It was good to see you." I turned to go back to the house and grab my clutch and keys. "I've got to work."

"Still working for Meme?" Mrs. Hubbard asked, shaking the bouquet at me.

"Yes, ma'am. It's a family business." I strolled closer to my house, making more distance between me and Mrs. Hubbard. If I didn't, she'd start asking questions I didn't want to answer.

"You tell that mom of yours that I'm going to give her a run for her money on the Hidden Treasure Tour," she warned.

"I'll do that." I ran up the front stairs and slammed the front door when I got safely inside. "Mom!" I yelled down the hall. "You better step up your garden game." I laughed and grabbed my keys and clutch off the counter. Mom had put the bundle of herbs next to them so I wouldn't forget to take them to The Brew. "Mrs. Hubbard is going to give you a run for your money."

Mom stopped plucking the herbs and looked at me. There wasn't a bit of amusement in her eyes. She took her life's journey very seriously.

I put my arms up in the air with my hands stuffed. "Her words not mine." I winked and headed out the back door. "Hey, do you think I could take more of an active role in cooking at the diner?"

Mom's head snapped back, she took me in.

"I'm so tired of not having a purpose." I objected to her stare. "I know the Witchy Hour and stuff, but I'm twenty-eight years old and I'd like to get on with my life."

"When you have your Witchy Hour, your life will get on," she said and went back to plucking.

"Mom." I cried, getting her attention. "All I'm asking is for you to talk to Auntie Meme and tell her you agree to let me have a more active role in the kitchen."

"Maybe." She shrugged, pointing to the door for me to get going.

Mom had really done an amazing job in our back yard. We had a play pool; it was only four feet deep and not very long, but it was big enough for the four of us to get in and enjoy on a hot Kentucky summer day. Plus the vibrant colors of the flower garden Mom had grown along with special herbs made the yard pop with colors. The fountain that drained into a curvy pond where koi fish lived was a new feature. Mrs. Hubbard hadn't seen it and was going to probably die right there while the tour was going on. That wasn't my concern. I had to get to work before Auntie Meme had her own heart attack.

I used the keypad to open the electric garage door.

"Good morning, Vinnie," I said to my 1965 red AC Cobra familiar.

His lights blinked off and on, the driver door swung open, and the engine started.

"Good morning, Maggie. I hope you find the temperature to your liking this cool morning," Vinnie said, as he always aimed to please me.

I got in and put the herbs down on the passenger seat along with my purse.

"I see your mom has been busy this morning."

"She has." I shut the door and put my hands on the wheel. "What's the weather today?"

"A cold front is coming through and will be here for the next couple of days." Vinnie pulled out, taking a right down the alley.

At the end, he took another right on Sixth Street and then a left on Hill Street.

"I imagine you will be busy today." Vinnie was good at making small talk.

He hadn't had to get me out of too many bad situations. And I wasn't sure what he could do as my familiar to keep me safe. But I never questioned. He was a cool car and he had become more of a friend than a car. Sounded strange, but it was true.

"I hope so," I groaned. "You know," I sighed. "I'm twenty-eight and I don't want to be stuck in a diner all my life." I bit my lip wondering if I was going to have to create my own destiny and not worry about what my heritage said my life's journey was. "Or maybe we have become so engrained in the mortal world, we don't have a life's journey anymore."

"You mean like an evolution type of theory?" Vinnie asked pulling up to the curb on Fourth Street where the diner was located.

"Yeah. Something like that. Something has got to give or I'm going to find my own journey. Create my own Witchy Hour." I sucked in a deep breath and looked through The Brew's front windows.

It was already busy. Many of the regulars were already bellied up to the counter.

"You leave well enough alone. Your Witchy Hour will be here soon enough." Vinnie didn't like me messing with the spirits. "You are messing with your future and that is not up to you."

Contrary to what mortals lived by, *you can be anything you want to be*, not me. I had to be what I was destined to be and I knew in my gut The Brew wasn't my destiny.

I grabbed the bundle of herbs and my clutch and opened the door to get out. Once I got out, I glanced around to make sure no one saw me talking to my car. I bent down into the driver's side and said, "I'll see you in a few hours."

I shut the door and watched Vinnie zoom down Fourth before I stepped up onto the sidewalk in front of the diner.

The Brew, our family-owned retro style diner, was a great cover for my family's little secret in Louisville, Kentucky. The residents here loved Kentucky basketball and fast horses, not a family full of witches. I'm not sure how or why my mom and Auntie Meme came to live in Kentucky, but it's been home to me all my life.

We fit in. Mom made sure of it. While growing up, during the day Lilith and I went to an all girls school and at night we went to witchery school. Witchery school was taught by Auntie Meme and Mom in our living room.

We had the latest and greatest clothes. With a flick of my hand, I could make an old rag look like a runway dress. Lilith was the true stylist. In fact, Lilith went to real cosmetology school at a local mortal school after high school. Auntie Meme thought it was great. Mom, on the other hand, thought it was disastrous. Lilith was a sloppy witch and Mom knew it. If Lilith messed up a client's hair or nails, she'd whip her hand in the air fixing it with magic. If the client knew it, Lilith would wipe their memory and a whole new set of problems would occur. Me, I stayed on the straight and narrow.

Sure I did my fair share of what we called fun spells, like the whole dare thing Lilith and I played with each other, but other than those, I was on the straight path. My own words tumbled around in my head. Was I destined to take over The Brew?

About the Author

For years, *USA Today* bestselling author Tonya Kappes has been self-publishing her numerous mystery and romance titles with unprecedented success. She is famous not only for her hilarious plotlines and quirky characters, but her tremendous marketing efforts that have earned her thousands of followers and a devoted street team of fans. Be sure to check out Tonya's website for upcoming events and news and to sign up for her newsletter! Tonyakappes.com

Also by Tonya Kappes

Olivia Davis Paranormal Mystery Series
SPLITSVILLE.COM
COLOR ME LOVE (novella)
COLOR ME A CRIME

Magical Cures Mystery Series
A CHARMING CRIME
A CHARMING CURE
A CHARMING POTION (novella)
A CHARMING WISH
A CHARMING SPELL
A CHARMING MAGIC
A CHARMING SECRET
A CHARMING CHRISTMAS (novella)
A CHARMING FATALITY
A CHARMING GHOST
A CHARMING HEX
A CHARMING VOODOO

Spies and Spells Mystery Series
SPIES AND SPELLS
BETTING OFF DEAD
GET WITCH OR DIE TRYING

Grandberry Falls Series
THE LADYBUG JINX
HAPPY NEW LIFE
A SUPERSTITIOUS CHRISTMAS (novella)
NEVER TELL YOUR DREAMS

A Laurel London Mystery Series

CHECKERED CRIME
CHECKERED PAST
CHECKERED THIEF

A Divorced Diva Beading Mystery Series
A BREAD OF DOUBT SHORT STORY
STRUNG OUT TO DIE
CRIMPED TO DEATH

Bluegrass Romance Series
GROOMING MR. RIGHT
TAMING MR. RIGHT

Women's Fiction
CARPE BREAD 'EM

Young Adult
TAG YOU'RE IT

A Ghostly Southern Mystery Series
A GHOSTLY UNDERTAKING
A GHOSTLY GRAVE
A GHOSTLY DEMISE
A GHOSTLY MURDER
A GHOSTLY REUNION
A GHOSTLY MORTALITY

Kenni Lowry Mystery Series
FIXIN' TO DIE

Copyright

Made in the USA
Lexington, KY
29 October 2016